"THE PERFECT
HUMOR BOOK
FOR THE DIRTY
OLD MAN IN
YOUR LIFE."
—*Camden (N.J.) Courier-Post*

Everything You Never Wanted To Know About Sex

by Sol Weinstein

PAPERBACK LIBRARY

A KINNEY SERVICE COMPANY
NEW YORK

PAPERBACK LIBRARY EDITION

First Printing: March, 1971
Second Printing: April, 1971
Third Printing: May, 1971
Fourth Printing: June, 1971
Fifth Printing: October, 1971

Copyright © 1971 by Sol Weinstein
All rights reserved

Lines from the song "Jack, Jack, Jack" used by permission of Barton Music Corporation.

Paperback Library is a division of Coronet Communications, Inc. Its trademark, consisting of the words "Paperback Library" accompanied by an open book, is registered in the United States Patent Office. *Coronet Communications, Inc., 315 Park Avenue South, New York, N.Y. 10010.*

DEDICATIONS

ELLIE, my beloved wife * DAVID and JUDY, my beloved children * SAM and CHAI SOORA WEINSTEIN, my beloved parents * HARRY and BESS EISNER, my in-laws * MR. and MRS. STAN EISNER * DR. and MRS. HOWARD FRIEDMAN * HOWARD and BERNICE ALBRECHT * SHELDON KELLER, "A Man and His Mishegaas" * JACK McKINNEY, who is either in the Sinn Fein or the Shinbet at the moment; author of the lilting song, "Whenever they got his Irish up, Clancy lowered his drawers. . . ." * RONN OWENS of WKAT, Miami, so young, so brash—so what? * ALLAN and WANDA DRAKE * MILTON BERLE * JOEY and SYLVIA BISHOP * LOUIE NYE * TIMMIE (Oh Yeah!) ROGERS * ART (Dah dah dah dah, dah dah dah) METRANO and WALLY AMOS * JOE E. LEWIS, who exemplifies grace under alcoholism * JACKIE KANNON, America's No. 1. "Ratfink," a comedian not to be missed! * MARK RUSSELL. *

JOSH SHERMAN and the Santa Monica Post Office * JAKE SHERMAN * CLARA SHERMAN * JACK SHERMAN and DR. YEHUDAH SHERMAN * JACK and SOPHIE ROSENBERG * EARL WILSON * NORTON MOCKRIDGE * CHARLES McHARRY * CHARLES PETZOLD * FRANK BROOKHOUSER * JEROME AGEL * FRANK FARRELL * TEX McCRARY * NORMAN SHAVIN * BEVERLEY GITHENS * ART HOPPE * JOE FRANKLIN * GARY OWENS and GEOFF EDWARDS of KMPC, Los Angeles * HARRY HARRIS * ROSE (SAM) DEWOLFE * "COUSIN DAVE" and ROSALIE GOMBERG * KEN GARLAND * KEN ARTIS * IRVING SHURACK * RON FRIEDMAN * FRED FREEMAN * BILL LINK and DICK LEVINSON * SAM and PEGGY RUDOFKER * BOB SCHILLER * CAROLE AXE * BOBBY WEINER * NOEL BLANC * TANIA GROSSINGER *

"SWEET DICK" WHITTINGTON * WINK MARTINDALE * TOM BROWN * PAUL COMPTON * LARRY VAN NUYS and CHUCK SOUTHCOTT of KGIL, San Fernando, Calif. * HARVEY KURTZMAN * LES and GAIL ROBERTS of Sherman Oaks, Calif. * PAUL GRAY

JACK CARTER * JAN MURRAY * MORTY GUNTY * LOHMAN and BARKLEY of KFI, Los Angeles * DAVE BARRY * E. WILLIAM MANDEL * MICHAEL JACKSON of KABC, Los Angeles * ARNAE SULTAN * GORDON FARR and ARNOLD KANE * CLEVELAND AMORY * JERRY GAGHAN * HERB RAU * HERB KELLY * JESS CAIN and LENNY MEYERS of WHDH, Boston * AUSTIN and IRMA KALISH * JOHN O. DOWNEY * JACK CLEMENTS * JOHN FACENDA * ANDY MUSSER * JOEL A. SPIVAK * ED. HARVEY * DOM QUINN * BERNIE HERMAN * J. J. SCOTT * AUSTIN CULMER * BILL HART * TOM BROOKSHIRE * DON FISHER * DAN STREETER * and the lovable, rib-tickling AL JULIUS of WCAU Radio-TV, Philadelphia. "Hi, Sol Weinstein here on two-way radio "where conversation makes aggravation. What's that, sir? I'm a dirty *what?* And I should do *what* to myself? An interesting suggestion for self-reproduction and thanks for your call. Now a word about Pagano's Restaurant. . . ." * PETE (THE BARON) RETZLAFF "No, fellas, not house, house, house. It's hut, hut, hut. . . ." *

RABBIS WILLIAM FIERVERKER, BENJAMIN SINCOFF and MELVIN GOLDSTINE, and CANTOR YEHUDAH KELLER * BOB and HOWIE TEDDER * TOM DUNPHY * JACK and JOAN CONDON * DAVID and BOBBIE TIDUS * SAUL and GRACE BASS * IRV and MAL COHEN * JACK FINSTON * LARRY and ANN KRUSS * HARVEY and ANNE LEVINE * KEN and BEV LEVINE * MICKEY and SHARON WERSH * SID and SALLY HERSHFIELD * PAUL (THE TARZANA KID) HERSHFIELD * BURT and SHIRLEY RITTER * HANK and BARBARA KATES * GENE RODGERS * SAM AROUESTY * JANINE JACOBY * SANDY BARNETT * IRV and BEV PEDOWITZ * ABE and JEAN FRIEDMAN * LEON, CLAIRE and KIRK NUROCK * MEL and MARGE LIFSON * TOM and BETTY BRENEMAN * GEORGE and KARIN BREITWIESER * MR. and MRS. RICHARD READ * ALICE HELGESON * MARVIN and NORMA GATES * BOB and SHIRLEY ROBERTS * BOB and JOAN STULMAN * SAM and JANET PEARL * CLYDE LEIB * RAY HASSON * BEN BOROWSKY * TOM DURAND * LADDIE SCHAEFER * JOHNNY COATS SR. and JR. * SYLVIA WEINSTOCK * LARRY and BETTY WAGREICH *

SID MARK, GEORGE LYLE and STEWART CHASE, of WWDB-FM, Philadelphia * ELIN BELSKY * LINDA GALLO * JOANNE O'DONNELL * DON BARNETT * RANDY WOOD * LEN and NORA FISCHMAN * EDDIE and ALICE GREENBERG * DORA KAPLAN * ANN ROSSER * ARNIE and SANDRA SIMON * STEVE and JANET LEVINSON * SOL, HELEN and HANNAH RATNOFSKY * ROSE and ELYSE RUDOW * RICHARD and RICKI RUDOW * BENNY and JENNY LINDENBAUM * EVA, SID and CHARLOTTE LINDENBAUM * IZ and JENNIE KRAKOWER * DR. KEN and MARTY SCHWARTZ * HESHY and DORIS HOROWITZ * FRED and NETTIE BERK * PHYLLIS

FISCHMAN * CHARLES and BELLA GREENBERG * CY and CLAIRE NEIBURG * RAY and BEA BARNETT * PETER REMENY * SID and ESTELLE LUTZKER * HARRY BOTOFF * NEIL LEVENSON * BERNIE GOLDBERG * MARK LITOWITZ * IRWIN and HERB SPIEGEL * WALT and MATTI MYERS * REGINA TELLEZ * JULIUS (YUDEL) KAPLAN * MARV and PHYLLIS HABAS * DOUG CHINA * WALT CANTER * MIKE and MARILYN ROSENFELD * ARNOLD BIEGEN, esq. * MENDY, WILLIE and DAVE KRAVITZ * STEVE SCHENKEL * MELVIN L. KARTZMER * DR. HERMAN CORN * DR. JULES SOBEL * JAMES R. LOWELL * HANNAH GRATZ * ROSARA BERMAN * BILLY GARBER * JEFF KELLER * FRANK SADOFSKY * BEN MELZER * STAN LEDERMAN * MARGE and MARIO PASCUCCI * MRS. MARY GENTILE * DON PALMER * MARV and MARSHA ROSENBERG * LIPPY and SYLVIA EISNER * JACK CURTIS * SAM and BOOTSI COLODNY * SALI HELLER * SID SHLAK * CHARLIE TRESKY * DAVE HORWITZ * CHICK and GLORIA HALFON * MARTIN and MIRIAM LAIBOW * MOLLY LEVINE * MICKEY DANER * GEORGE COHEN *

WILLIAM B. WILLIAMS of WNEW, N.Y. * ROBERT and VICKI LANE * NAT and MONICA SCHWARTZ * ALAN HARRIS * ARI and SHULAMITH RUTKOFF * AL and THELMA BARON * ART AZARCHI * LEW and EVELYN MARSHALL * LEN and ABBY FEINBERG * BARRY SNYDER * MR. and MRS. ART ABRAMSOHN * ROBERT PINCUS * GWENDA TALENS * HAROLD STRAUSE * JOE and CHARLOTT NASSAU * JERRY HIMMEL * MARTY SAVAR * ANDY FLAGER * BARRY REISMAN * JACK HELSEL * J. WELLINGTON PIDCOCK of WBCB, Levittown, Pa. * ISRAEL (COKE) RUBIN * BOB and JANE AMOROS * JACKIE HODES * ALLAN and WALLY PLAPINGER * ED CHELLAND * RON POLAO * IRV WURZEL * DR. SEYMOUR and RUTHE LEDIS * FRAN SHANKIN * TED and SYBIL COOPER * DR. MILTON PALAT * DR. GEORGE ISAACSON * DR. DONALD LUBER * SAUL ROSSIEN * BILL GERVON * WILLIAM H. PETTIT * NORM and MARGIE WEINSTEIN * BILL and LIL HOLSTEIN * FRANK and SUSIE MARRERO * ARNIE and PAT SOMERS * MILTON and EVE LEVINE * BOBBY and MONA COURTNEY * NORM LEIGHTON * BOB GOLDMAN *

DICK WEST of UPI * HORACE GREELY McNAB * WALT and LILLIAN LAMOND * WALLY and AUSTINE WARREN * LEN and HELEN BOGARDE * DR. and MRS.

LEWIS HIRSH * DOLLY COHEN * DAVE and HOPE WISNIA * STAN and JAN FEINTUCH * LINDA LATZ * HARVEY and HARRIET BLATT * NATALIE FULTON * ALAN and GRACE BRESLAU * HAL LEFCOURT * LOU, RUTH and ALLEN DELIN * JAMES E. MAGEE * BUS SAIDT * LAURA LANE * ROGER YAGER * SID and BUNNY SHORE * BOB CRAIG * MICHAEL SPOLL * ISADORE SOLOVAY * SID and RUTH SCHUCKER * MARTY MOSKOWITZ * DON SCOTT * EARL JOSEPHSON * FLORENCE BLOCK * CHARLES E. SCOTT * ART MOGER * TOM SNYDER of KNBC-TV, Los Angeles * BOB and ADELE HOGAN * ARNIE and CAROL BERNSTEIN * AL and FRANCES HEYMAN * MORRIS and ADRIENNE BERENBAUM * LOUIE and YETTA CRAVITZ * SAM and CEIL CRAVITT * YOUIE and CHARLOTTE CAPILUPI * GERRY and SELMA GOULD * LEN and DEBBIE SHAPIRO * LEN and FRAN ROSENFIELD * FLORENCE FRIEDMAN * TATSUJI NAGASHIMA * JAY STEVENS of WGBS, Miami * JOHN WINGATE *

EMIL SLABODA * HARVEY YAVENER * ED "DUFFY" RAMSEY * STEVE MERVISH * JOE LOGUE and GEORGE MOLDOVAN, of *The Trentonian,* Trenton, N.J. * ED and KAREN BROWN * LEON BROWN, of the Philadelphia *Jewish Exponent* * JAMES J. SHAPIRO, of Simplicity Patterns * FORREST DUKE * RALPH PEARL * BOB JOYCE, of KRAM, Las Vegas * AL FELDSTEIN and NICK MEGLIN, of Mad Magazine * JACK WALSH, the world's strongest beer drinker * EDDIE GOLDEN * ABEL GREEN and NORMA NANNINI, of *Variety* * BOB MENEFEE * JAMES GARRETT, of the *Cleveland Press* * JOSEPH P. MUNIZ * GEORGE BOURKE, of the *Miami Herald* * LARRY KING * WAYNE ROBINSON * A. C. SPECTORSKY, SHELLY WAX, MURRAY FISHER and JULI BAINBRIDGE, of *Playboy* * MARUCA'S TOMATO PIES * of Trenton, N.J. * SAM JACOBS, of *American Jewish Life,* Trenton, N.J. * DR. BERNARD and RHODA AMSTER * LARRY DeVINE, wherever you are . . ." GEORGE SPOTA * CLARENCE PETERSON * REGIS PHILBIN * ROBERT SCHEERER * DON VAN ATTA * GENE DINOVI * TONY VELONA * ANITA MANN * ARLENE SIDARIS * ANNE MENNA * MELISSA GREENE * GREG PITZER * YVONNE WILDER * . . . and WILBUR and NANCY BROWN LEVINE of Poughkeepsie, N.Y. *

Finally, to my glorious body, without whose incandescent lust this book never could have been written.

CHAPTER ONE

KNOW THE TRUTH, AND IT SHALL MAKE YOU HORNEY

Why?
Why another sex book on a market already glutted by the outpourings of tongue-flicking, hip-swiveling "sensuous women" and owl-eyed professors puffing meerschaums full of tweed, all of whom purport to know the path to absolute sexual fulfillment?

Let Miss Y.C., who told me she had read every single one of these books and yet was batting .000 in the boudoir, be my living argument for the publication of this admittedly slim, but invaluable, volume.

When she lurched into my clinic that August afternoon, Y.C. was a twitching mass of anxiety. Gentleman that I am, I offered my hand in greeting, but hers eluded it and darted straight for my Talon zipper, a clear indication to a trained observer of her specific fixation. As she nervously chainsmoked one ballpoint pen after another, Y.C. seemed incapable of concentrating on my routine queries about her age, occupation, familial history, education, etc., mindlessly answering each one with the four-letter vulgarism for the word "fornication":

"Forn!"
"Forn!"
"Forn!"

As I jotted down my initial impressions of her psychological state, Y.C. undulated her tightly packed buttocks against the pelvic area of a statuette of Apollo, which responded by displaying an eye-popping erection. (I have since begun to treat the statuette.)

After I immersed her in a tub of tepid Knox Gelatin and massaged her with a heated English muffin, she relaxed enough to let down her guard and Little Prune Panty-hose and confessed freely. A few days before our appointment, she said, she had decided to yield her favors to a man for the first time in her 36 years on this planet. (Subsequent interrogation revealed she had also spent 77 years on another planet, but this is not relevant to my narrative.)

To accomplish her amatory aim Y.C. had transformed her $150-a-month efficiency apartment into a bower of seduction. The lights had been lowered by ramming a tire iron into the cellar circuitbreakers; a provocative scent of Easy-Off oven spray floated suggestively over her Simmons hide-a-bed; his favorite repast, *enchiladas de gato,* served thoughtfully with a side dish of Diet Kaopectate, had been received with lip-smacking gusto, and a moody long-playing album, "Minne Pearl's Memories of Woodstock," whirred an unmistakable invitation to love.

Then—catastrophe.

"Oh, Dr. Weinstein, I really meant to have the experience, really I did. But then some of the crazy notions I'd picked up at senior high pajama parties with the girls started to haunt me. Just the thought of Courtney pushing his peanuts into my virginia made me recoil. My aretha* tightened up and pushed down on my plethora, which was anathema to me. Courtney noticed my uneasiness and, I must say, was pretty decent about it. He suggested that, if I couldn't have regular sexual innertube, at least I should practice *horatio* or *feliciano* on him and he, in turn, would do *cunneiform* on me. But I couldn't do that either, so

* The gland discovered by Dr. Franklin.

poor Courtney relieved himself by mastication and left in a Huff, his German sportscar, and I haven't seen him since."

Lest there be those among my readership tempted to sneer at Y.C.'s abysmal garbling of anatomical references, let me add quickly that she is no backwoods dolt, but rather an attractive, cultured individual who can discourse knowingly on a variety of topics from nuclear global annihilation (which she favors) to legalization of marijuana (which she opposes on the grounds it would weaken the moral fabric of society).

But in one crucial area, that bounded by her finely fleshed, supple thighs and saucy, throbbing pubis (if the reader desires to masticate at this point, it is quite permissible), she is a veritable Sesame Street toddler; nay, not even that, because at least Sesame Street watchers would know exactly what to do with a Big Bird.

Y.C. is by no means alone in her tragic ignorance. All too often in the course of my consultative sessions have I heard patients use similar malapropisms:

"Doctor, I can't bear the idea of his pennants unfurling in my angina. It must be agony!"

Or: "He should rupture my hymie with his penitents? Not on your life."

And, in the case of a male patient: "Doc, before we indulge in . . . well, you know . . . why does my wife always send me on these wild goose chases? Nobody at Seven-Eleven's dairy counter ever *heard* of Ortho-Creme. . . ."

One needs only to multiply Y.C. and her genitally illiterate ilk by untold millions of fellow citizens to obtain a depressing picture of an America up to its morass in sexual ineptitude

None of this is my fault. Indeed, had my earlier texts received as much publicity and attention as those ground out by the fast-buck sex book artists who have dominated the best-seller lists for the last ten years, our entire citizenry would be delighting in mega-orgasm after mega-orgasm. U.S.A. would signify Utterly Satisfied America.

My qualifications as an expert in the field of sex were derived not from musty books but from the pragmatic experience gained in that noblest of all academies —the School of Hard Knockers. They are the direct result of my establishment of and involvement in the Clinic for Unrepressed Navel Titillation, perhaps better known by either its catchy acronym or the more informal name, the Green Peacock Motel, located on Route One, Lawrence Township, New Jersey (ask for Renzo DeLuca). In the Green Peacock's aromatic, friendly cubicles I observed, and often participated with, the lay public, and long before Masters and Johnson even conceived the idea of filming couples in coitus as a visual aid, I was using videotape, Instant Replay, isolated cameras and color analysts.

Intensive scrutiny of the sexual activities of the motel's clientele (they dubbed themselves the John Smith Society) led me to the authoring of a solid, informative series of manuals: *Can There Be Sex After Marriage?*, *"Bring New Excitement Into Your Marriage by Cheating*, *Sex Without Shame*, *Sex Without Guilt*, *Sex Without A Partner* (whose major theme was cribbed brazenly by Phillip Roth for his *Portnoy's Complaint*), *Sexual Variations for Alcoholics: Hot Toddy on a Hot Body*, and the sado-masochist classic, *Happiness Is A Warm Whip*.

Alas, the major foundations of this country, operated in the main by the anti-erotic, desiccated descendants of Puritans, chose to ignore my innovative techniques and instead bankrolled the stodgy researchers whose prissy attitudes have steered an ordinarily robust, free-spirited American people to their lamentable sexual dead end. It is not necessary to single out these "experts" by name. One sees them constantly on late night TV shows peddling their shopworn theories. But merely looking at their parchment-like complexions, slack jaws and muddy eyes convinces the viewer these chalatans have known physical ecstasy as often as Abby Hoffman has been tendered the Man of the Year award by the Veterans of Foreign Wars.

But fortune has smiled upon me, albeit belatedly. I have now found a leading publisher willing to expose me to the general public—much as I myself have been doing for years—and it is to be hoped that *EVERYTHING YOU NEVER WANTED TO KNOW ABOUT SEX, BUT I'LL TELL YOU ANYWAY* reaches a vast audience in desperate need of the nitty-gritty.

A few Kudos are in order. My secretary, Louella Soames-Forsyte, earns my heartfelt gratitude for the many times she burned the midnight oil in my den proofreading the manuscript. Because midnight oil is quite a volatile, unstable substance, on two occasions she burned the manuscript and the den, but I commend her for her efforts and for her heartwarming analysis of these pages: "Doctor, it's the first time I've ever been knocked up by a book." Further thanks are due my wife for her frequent prolonged absences from home, which cleared the way for frequent, prolonged consultations with Miss Fannette DuPree of Reseda, California, one of the San Fernando Valley's most sought after sexual therapists. A thoroughly unpretentious young woman, Miss DuPree prefers to refer to her vocation by its down-to-earth nomenclature: hooker.

Brief thanks, too, to my attorneys, Parsley, Sage, Rosemary & Thyme, for negotiating with the publisher; to Pierre LeFoux and his gallant croux who cut down the trees providing the paper pulp for this edition, and to the hardworking Najeewah River for carrying thousands of logs to the mill, despite a persistent and painful sciatic condition.

Here then, labias and genitals of my reading audience, is *EVERYTHING YOU NEVER WANTED TO KNOW ABOUT SEX, BUT I'LL TELL YOU ANYWAY*. Its format is simple. Questions about sex are posed to me; I answer them fearlessly, straight from the thighs. For I believe if you know the truth about sex it will make you free. And horny. And that's good.

Crotches of the world, unite! You have nothing to lose but a few hours away from prime-time television. And *that's* good.

Camarillo, California
December, 1970.

CHAPTER TWO

SEX: AN AMERICAN TRAGEDY

DOCTOR, HOW LONG HAS MANKIND BEEN INVOLVED IN SEX?

At least as far back as the Pleistocene Age. We know our earliest ancestors were capable of erotic manifestations from examining the remains of one discovered in the volcanic rock of Java. Blushing anthropologists gave the creature the rather polite Latinate designation of "Pithecanthropus Erectus."

WHICH MEANS?

Caveman with an erection. Poor chap; just as he was about to enjoy an eruption, the volcano beat him to it. Seeing that incredible spurt of lava must have given him a horrible feeling of inadequacy.

Many of the religions of antiquity celebrated sex in story and song, the Eastern ones going so far as to depict graphic scenes of multifarious sexual activities in carvings on the exterior walls of their houses of worship. It was an elephant driver who, coursing with desire after perusing for many hours the cuddling, caressing, cohabiting carvings, coined the phrase: "It's enough to drive a guy up the wall!" While the world should pay the utmost respect to the Wailing Wall of the Middle East, there certainly is something to be said for the Balling Wall of the Far East. To this day temple attendance in Southeast Asia remains at a high level, and the United Hindu Appeal always makes its quota.

DOES THIS INDICATE THAT SEX AND RELIGION ARE COMPATIBLE?

To answer that I need only quote a poem inscribed on the archway to an ancient temple in Burma!

> Sex and religion go hand in hand,
> So it isn't very odd,
> To ball a broad in the jungle night,
> And to hear her sigh, "Oh, God!"
> Burma Shave.

WE CAN COMPREHEND FROM WHAT YOU'VE TOLD US THAT SEX CAME NATURALLY AND FREELY TO FAR EASTERN PEOPLES, BUT WHY DO WE IN AMERICA HAVE SUCH TERRIBLE SEX HANGUPS?

Basically because we've been victimized by the sorry heritage left us by those pitiful Puritans and Pilgrims alluded to earlier, whose anti-sexualism continues to distort the love lives of the overwhelming majority of Americans. Yet how can one blame those rugged pioneers for harboring such attitudes, considering what they had to face?

To begin with, they were fleeing the persecution of the deranged King George the Third of England, never knowing when his minions might catch up to them and inflict cruel punishment. The only transportation available was on rolling, pitching boats like the Mayflower. Leaning over the rail for three months, racked by constant nausea, who could enjoy sex? On that ship a Pilgrim could neither keep anything down nor up. The relentless, inimical Atlantic, thrashing to and fro, hurled its icy waters into the hold. One chilling twenty-foot wave pounding over your navel and you wouldn't be a Paul Newman, either! Then when they landed on New England's forbidding shores, what did they find? A vicious climate fraught with more bone-paralyzing cold, more teeth-chattering gales. Savage Indians lurked about their drafty cabins by night whooping hideous war cries. Some nights the only meaningful penetration was by arrow. And those accursed turkeys outside, interrupting the most intimate moments with their strident gobble, gobble, gobble! Even if a Pilgrim woman somehow forced every single one of these distractions from her mind, how could she take seriously a proposition from a man in a funny hat with little faggot buckles on his shoes?

BUT, DOCTOR, THESE SEXUALLY REPRESSIVE EVENTS OCCURRED CENTURIES AGO. WHY SHOULD THEY BE OF PARAMOUNT INFLUENCE TODAY?

Because the Pilgrims and Puritans handed down these horrific stories to their offspring, who, in turn, passed them along to theirs. Thus, to this day the average American WASP remains conditioned by the terrors of the past. No matter where he may be—in a resort hotel in Fort Lauderdale, a rustic lodge in the Rockies or on a surfboard in Malibu—he still can not find delectation in his sex life. In the very midst of intercourse he feels the swaying of the Mayflower with its concomitant nausea, he hears the war whoops and whistling arrows of the savages, the ear-splitting gobbling of the turkeys, and, worse, he fully expects the vindictive King George and his brutal Redcoats to break in on him at any second.

AT MALIBU?

They could be crouched on the very next surfboard, ready to spring at him.

CAN YOU DO ANYTHING TO HELP THE WASP AND OTHER FRUSTRATED PEOPLES ATTAIN SEXUAL GRATIFICATION?

Yes, but only by discussing sex in an open and aboveboard manner. To begin with, let us examine the human body, that masterpiece of intricate construction from "The Great Hard Hat in the Sky."

CHAPTER THREE

THE MALE: THE HANG OF IT

WHAT IS THE PENIS?

The penis, in the deathless words of Ovid, the Roman Rod McKuen, is "the lollipop of love." Catullus, another classical poet, saw it as "the carnal candle, the unmeltable suppository, the only genuine goldenrod." A Judaic philosopher immortalized it in his sensuous love ballad, "The Prong of Prongs." In our own era certain officials in the top echelons of law enforcement have called it "a tool of the International Communist Conspiracy."

WHAT ARE ITS FUNCTIONS?

It is the male organ for sexual pleasure and urination. These functions ninety-nine times out of a hundred are performed separately, but in the rare instance where, due to inexplicable scrambling of tubes, ducts and nerves, they occur simultaneously, the effect can be disastrous. A man thus afflicted can literally be said to be piddling away his love life.

Dangling from the pelvic area, the penis performs yet another valuable function. It keeps the inner thighs from colliding too frequently and hence retards chapping. Cylindrical in shape, the penis supports the fleshy pouch housing the testicles called the scrotum. Indian tribes of America's Northwest venerated the organ by etching huge replicas of it from tree trunks, which they called "scrotum poles."

HOW LONG SHOULD THE PENIS BE?

Once, as he stood outside the Parthenon in Athens waiting for the nine o'clock show to break, the immortal Socrates was asked, "How long should a man's legs be?" Socrates reflected for a moment, smiled and replied: "Just long enough to reach the ground."

A LOGICAL ENOUGH ANSWER FOR THE LEGS, BUT HOW LONG SHOULD THE PENIS BE?

Just long enough to reach the ground.

THAT SEEMS TO BE A BIT OF WISHFUL THINKING ON YOUR PART. IN GENERAL, THOUGH, WHAT IS THE NORMAL SIZE OF THE PENIS?

It can range in length from six inches (or 150 millimeters, in case a man is having relations with a European woman whose vagina, of course, would be on the metric system) to two feet.

A PENIS CAN BE TWO FEET?

If it's the penis of a Cape Buffalo. Which, incidentally, accounts for the increasing number of Boston spinsters signing up for safaris and a distinct unhappiness on the faces of Great White Hunters.

IS THAT THE LARGEST PENIS IN THE ANIMAL WORLD?

Hardly. A rhino's may be three feet, an elephant's four feet, and the greatest of all the seven-footer wielded by the whale. (A psychological study of Herman Melville's novel *Moby Dick*—and how transparently sexual that title is!—suggests that Captain Ahab's outward hatred of the great white whale cloaked a secret homosexual yearning for Moby and that the mammoth mammal nurtured a similar affection for his pursuer. The shouted phrase "thar she blows!" is, of course, the dead giveaway.)

IN YOUR OWN EXPERIENCE, WHAT'S THE LARGEST ORGAN YOU'VE EVER SEEN?

The Wurlitzer at the old Roxy Theater in New York. You see, even serious-minded sexual experts can crank out a one-liner now and then!

HOW DO WOMEN FEEL ABOUT THE SIZE OF A MAN'S PENIS?

With their fingers, of course.

ACTUALLY WE MEANT—HOW DO WOMEN FEEL PSYCHOLOGICALLY ABOUT THE SIZE OF THE PENIS?

Women in pristine societies were taught to worship the penis of enormous length and diameter, which symbolized awesome masculinity and was supposed to guarantee orgasms on a Richter scale of 9.7. Today's sexually sophisticated woman, who has gleaned much information about the functions of the penis from medical journals, hence possesses far more knowledge on the subject than her sisters of old. Given a choice, penis-wise, between quantity and quality, she will make it on a scientific, not an emotional basis.

WHAT WILL SHE CHOOSE?

Quantity.

WAS FREUD RIGHT WHEN HE CONTENDED WOMEN HAD PENIS ENVY?

It has become *de rigueur* these days to pooh-pooh the theories of Sigmund Freud. But the old master's concept of penis envy in the female was right on the head. Women do have a feeling that somehow at birth they were defrauded of a penis. But if it were possible to wave a magic wand and present all women *with* a magic wand, what would happen? Knowing women as I do, the outcome would be yawningly predictable.

For a while they'd be quite satisfied with the penis as it stands, but then the inevitable female yen to be in the vanguard of high fashion would come to the fore. They'd become intrigued with the idea of improvisation. Some would begin dyeing the penis in all sorts of exotic colors—coral, fuschia, puce. Some would affix effulgent patent leather bows or twinkling sequins to it. There would be frilly penises with tiny holes bored in the testicles for raindrop earrings . . . bell-bottomed penises . . . "soul" penises framed by pubic hair allowed to grow "Afro" . . . severely tailored, mohair-clad penises for career girls . . . mini, midi and maxi penises. And ultimately some Louisiana belle would say petulantly, "Ah do decleah! This l'il ol' thang keeps gettin' in mah way whenevah Ah have sexual intuhco'se with mah beaus. Ah do believe Ah'm jes' gonna cut off the l'il buggah entirely and go on with the winnin' o' the South. . . ."

LET'S BE EVERLASTINGLY GRATEFUL THAT WOMEN DON'T HAVE PENISES AND GET BACK TO THOSE WHO DO. DOCTOR, ARE ALL MALE PENISES NORMAL IN SHAPE?

Ninety-nine and 44/100 per cent are, but there is the exceedingly rare penile distortion known as the Bent-Nail Syndrome.

WHAT CAUSES IT?

Scar tissue insidiously invades the shaft of the penis, despite repeated warnings from the United Nations, and when the man becomes erect in preparation for sexual penetration, weird things happen. The shaft of the penis may point northwest, but the head heads southeast. A man cursed by this condition should not even attempt intercourse unless he has a Rand McNally map at his bedside.

WE ARE TOLD LEADING MEDICAL AUTHORITIES BELIEVE THERE IS NO CURE FOR THE "BENT-NAIL SYNDROME." DO YOU AGREE?

Sometimes the astounding lack of imagination of my fellow colleagues makes me wince in embarrassment for the whole profession. Of course, there is a treatment, the same directed to any bent-nail configuration, penile or otherwise. One good, smashing blow from a Stanley hammer wielded by a skillful surgeon and, *voila!*, the organ is straight again. Such a treatment has its unpleasant minor side effects, such as the patient aging fifty years in one excruciating second, and a psychological one as well. A man who has been straightened out in this manner may go into convulsions upon passing a hardware store or hearing Peter, Paul & Mary's rendition of "If I Had A Hammer."

ARE THERE ANY OTHER MALADIES WHICH COULD THREATEN THE MALE EROGENOUS ZONE?

Just one other worth mentioning, but we on this side of the Atlantic needn't concern ourselves about it. I refer to elephantiasis, caused by a parasitic infection that balloons the testicles to the size of watermelons or beachballs. African tribesmen victimized by this grisly disease find their sex lives severely limited because their women flee from them in understandable horror. Occasionally, though, a female elephant with poor eyesight wanders by and that seems to lessen the tension somewhat. Incidentally, victims of elephantiasis must push their inflated genitals around in wheelbarrows, which has given rise to the annual Kenya "500" wheelbarrow race, surely one of the most unique events in athletic history. Someday, perhaps, the ABC television network will have the courage to carry it here as the "Extra-Wide Wide World of Sports."

NOW, DOCTOR WEINSTEIN, LET'S TALK ABOUT THE ROLE OF THE PENIS IN THE SEXUAL ACT. FIRSTLY, HOWEVER, WHAT CAUSES IT TO BE AROUSED?

Who can select from the myriads of visual, aural or tactile elements available to the senses of a man precisely those which cause his penis to stiffen? Perhaps the sight of fleecy clouds scudding across some awe-inspiring sunset or raw sewage rushing into the sea. The feeling of sixteen ounces of coleslaw cascading from a split carton into his lap. A Texas League double to right by Pete Rose. In my own case, a particularly poignant essay on welfare cheaters by William F. Buckley. Or something as bizarre and kinky as watching the female in the next apartment disrobing.

ASSUMING HE IS AROUSED, HOW DOES THE MALE KNOW THAT WHATEVER FEMALE HE IS WITH IS SIMILARLY AROUSED? AFTER ALL, HIS ERECTION IS QUITE EVIDENT, BUT SHE HAS NO SUCH SEXUAL MANIFESTATION?

He may get an inkling of her state of mind in a more subtle way. Little Freudian slips in her conversation may clue him. "Darling, for dinner tonight would you go for some Long Island fu—er—duckling? Served with a piece of aspic? Then maybe we'll have a nightcap of Vat 69, huh, sweetcakes?" Or later in the evening she may suggest some romantic recordings. "A little Sinatra? A little Tony Bennett? Or, better still, how's about a little Humperdinck?" (I have yet to comprehend what a "dinck" means.)

IF THE WOMAN IS RELUCTANT ABOUT HAVING SEXUAL RELATIONS, WHAT TECHNIQUES CAN A MAN EMPLOY TO CHANGE HER MIND?

At his fingertips, ready to be drawn upon whene'er he sees fit, is a vast storehouse of romantic poetry from the pens of Chaucer and Shakespeare, Shelley and Keats, Poe and Longfellow, Henry Gibson and

Nipsey Russell. Quoting a heady passage or two from these giants is well calculated to ignite a firestorm of ardor in the chest, breast or nest of any female.

I personally have used a verse from the "Rubaiyat," slightly altered to fit in with today's sexual honesty:

> A loaf of bread, a jug of wine and thou,
> Beside me in the wilderness—oh wow!
> So don't hold back, but give me all you've got,
> And I'll give you a Ruby and a Yacht.

A taint of commerciality is implicit in my version, but it works.

WHAT TECHNIQUES ARE AVAILABLE TO A MAN WHO IS ILL AT EASE WITH THE MUSE OF POETRY?

The non-verbal male has his methods too. A menacing snarl and a forefinger run across the edge of a butcher knife can prove well nigh irresistible.

WHAT TECHNICAL FUNCTIONS OCCUR WHEN A MAN EXPERIENCES AN ERECTION?

An erection is analogous to the launching of a guided missile. Indeed, the term ICBM, when applied to sex, means Inter-Course Blastoff Mechanism.

What we have here is a felicitous cooperation between the brain, the lower section of the spinal cord, the central nervous system and, of course, the penis.

Let us demonstrate exactly what takes place. Baxter

Featherfax, a stockbroker from New Rochelle, N.Y., sits alone in his study, having just witnessed his wife drive off to the beauty parlor. As he pores over the Wall Street Journal, Inga, his recently acquired Danish maid, undulates into the room. She is blond, blue-eyed, beautiful and bouncy. From time to time she bends over to tidy up here and there.

EYES: Cheez . . . look at the smorgasbord on them tables! Brain, you reading me loud and clear?

BRAIN: Imagine, three miles from the nearest bakery and still we've got a piece of Danish on our hands. Nervous System, you feeling what I feel?

NERVOUS SYSTEM: Man, I'm so nervous. . . .

SPINAL CORD: Me too, guys. I'm shaking so hard I just threw off a truss and three layers of Minit-Rub.

PENIS: Better tell the blood to start rushing to the warhead. Minus three minutes and counting. . . .

NERVOUS SYSTEM: Now hear this, blood! Man your Ejaculation Station!

FEATHERFAX: Inga, my dear, I've been meaning to ask you. . . .

INGA: Yah, yah, yah. I bane horny. . . .

BRAIN: Featherfax, you sure you ought to be doing this instead of reading your stock reports? After all, the market is in flux.

FEATHERFAX: When it comes to a choice between the market and me, *my* flux comes first!

INGA: Hurry, hurry! I Am Curious Yellow, Blue, Green, Ebony, Pink, Purple, Aqua. . . .

NERVOUS SYSTEM: Minus two minutes and counting! Now hear this, Penis. I'm causing those small balloon-like reservoirs under your skin to become engorged with blood.

PENIS: (singing) "Up, up and away . . . with my beautiful balloons. . ."

SPINAL CORD: Fellas, you still sure we should go through with this?

PENIS: What's the matter, Spinal Cord? Ain't you got no backbone?

BRAIN: Minus one minute and counting! Contact with Inga made!

INGA: Rah, rah, rah!
Ciss boom bah!
You've hit it, you've hit it!
Yah, yah, yah!

EARS: Achtung, achtung! Sound of car in driveway!

EYES: Wife home unexpectedly early from beauty parlor! Scrub the mission, Featherfax! Scrub the mission!

FEATHERFAX: Scrub your ass! Five, four, three, two, one. . . .

WIFE: Baxter! Aha, I caught you . . . !

FEATHERFAX, BRAIN, SPINAL CORD, NERVOUS SYSTEM, PENIS: Blastoff!

WIFE: What have you got to say about this seamy interlude, Baxter?

FEATHERFAX: (Sententiously) One small step for man, one giant alimony check for my wife.

WHAT WAS IT THAT MR. FEATHERFAX DARED EVERYTHING FOR, HIS MARRIAGE, HIS REPUTATION, HIS BUSINESS?

For that sublime and rewarding moment of sexual ecstasy—the ejaculation. At that mind-boggling instant his penis hurled out a sticky, warm substance called by many different names: semen, seminal fluid, ejaculate, or, more technically, penis butter.

HOW MUCH OF THIS MATERIAL DID HE EJACULATE?

About five or six jets worth. It can happen, however, that a man has a genuine sensation of having ejaculated, but nothing emerges from the penis. This phenomenon I call the Phantom Jet Syndrome.* All told, a man who engages in a fairly regular program of sex will expel in his lifetime as many as eighteen quarts of semen or, if he be an immoderate drinker, fourteen and a half fifths.

IS THERE ANY OTHER PHYSICAL SENSATION IN THE HUMAN BODY EQUIVALENT TO THE EJACULATION?

There is a reasonably close facsimile of that kind of explosive release, but those self-same, ultra-cautious sexual researchers, who have earned my everlasting contempt for what they have done to their fellow beings, typically have failed to inform you about it. It is that tickling sensation and subsequent mini-detonation: the sneeze.

For one reason or another many individuals are unable to function in the primary sex act. They desperately required some sort of outlet, so they stumble across this secondary form, find it pleasurable, simple and inexpensive, and they do it.

---

* Occurring often in Cairo, but officially denied by the government.

HOW DO THEY INDULGE IN THIS SECONDARY FORM?

By inducing the sneeze in a secret, shameful act termed noserbation. They insert a pinch of Cayenne pepper straight into the nose, irritate the sensitive nasal hairs and membranes with Q-Tips, rub their nostrils into crushed velvet sofas, deliberately seek employment in dusty coal mines or factories manufacturing harsh detergents, etc. One can readily spot the chronic noserbator from the extra-thick hair in his nostrils and the sly smile on his face.

Mother Nature frequently lends a helping hand. On days when the pollen count is at an abnormally high level, mass orgies break out. One must never pity the victim of hay fever. He has literally nosed his way into paradise.

AN INTERESTING SIDELIGHT ON SEXUALITY, DOCTOR, AND WE ARE GRATEFUL FOR IT. BUT GETTING BACK TO MORE TRADITIONAL INTERCOURSE, WHAT IS PREMATURE EJACULATION?

His spill before her thrill.

So excited is the male by what he is doing that he cannot exercise restraint over his thrusting, lusting penis. Suddenly it pops, stops and flops. The ungratified female waits, berates and hates. This deplorable lack of quality control earns her fierce contempt. If he does not immediately institute a time-motion study the romance is in deep trouble.

HOW CAN THE MAN CONTROL THIS DISHEARTENING PREMATURE EJACULATION?

I am a firm believer in giving credit where it is due, so I tip my fedora to brilliant humorist Woody Allen, whose perception in these matters comes close to matching mine. In discussing the premature ejaculation problem in his third comedy phonograph album on Capital Records, Master Allen states that to prolong the sex act he makes a supreme effort of mental will and blots the thought of the orgasm completely out of his mind—even while slithering toward it. How? He thinks of baseball players such as Willie Mays, Willie McCovey, Tom Haller, etc. I have refined this technique to an even more effective extent. While on the verge of a crashing orgasm, I expunge it from my mind by thinking about Woody Allen. With frightening immediacy the sex drive is eradicated. So, incidentally, are the other major drives: hunger, shelter, even the will to live.

ISN'T PREMATURE EJACULATION JUST ONE PHASE OF WHAT WE CALL IMPOTENCE?

Yes. Other manifestations of impotence, which can be defined as the failure of the male to perform his sexual function, are no erection at all, a semi-erection (or "soft-on," in the parlance of the street), erection without ejaculation, ejaculation without erection, taxation without representation. . . . The possibilities are unlimited. (I shall discuss impotence more fully in another chapter.)

CAN HORMONAL INJECTIONS HELP THE IMPOTENT?

Some men do respond to massive dosages of testosterone, progesterone and, in the special case of males of Sicilian lineage, minestrone. Care should be taken not to administer too much of the latter, however, because although the man may experience an interesting revival of his sex powers, he often ends up ejaculating escarole, chickpeas or okra.

ARE THERE ANY MECHANICAL DEVICES DESIGNED TO KEEP ALOFT THE PENIS?

At various times in history man has tinkered up some singularly ingenious contraptions to enable his fellows to walk softly and carry a big stick. In particular, the Oriental peoples have been innovators in this specialty, but their contrivances, albeit imaginative, have experienced serious drawbacks.

One of the earliest devices was a hollow bamboo tube into which the limp, uncooperative penis was shoved to keep it in a constant attitude of erection. Alas, one of the properties of bamboo is brittleness and it would shatter into fragments inside the very vagina it was designed to thrill. Ow Wee, a pain-racked, disillusioned Shanghai concubine, moments after a distressing session with the bamboo penis took out her brush and scroll and in ornate calligraphy set down the words to the mournful ballad, "Love Is a Many Splintered Thing."

Then came the Cambodian contribution to male rigidity, which consisted of cutting several slits in the penis into which they affixed little tinkling bells. This, too, ended in ignominy. One night a Cambodian husband came home from a hard day in the opium fields, heard a suspicious clangor and rushed into his boudoir to find his wife being serviced by an intruder inserting a penile version of Quasimodo's bells of Notre Dame. The frightened lover, obviously a man of imagination, tried to convince the irate husband he was merely the new Southeast Asia representative of the Good Humor ice cream company, but the husband, a man of ill humor, wouldn't buy it. One swipe of his kriss and no more bliss.

Last year, the Japanese, undisputed masters of electronics, constructed a transistor radio-like box whose electrodes were attached at the ends of the penis and the rectum. It was designed to keep the organ erect by means of electrical charges, and appeared to be a genuine breakthrough. But when the power was turned on, signaling a sort of sexual "Tora! Tora! Tora!"* to the male, the transistor device, in addition to pumping out penis-stiffening impulses, began to pump out the top forty hits it was pulling in from a Tokyo rock n' roll station. Upon hearing in quick succession the frenetic songs of Crosby, Stills, Nash & Young, the Creedence Clearwater Revival and Joe Cocker echoing inside her vagina (plus three Datsun commercials), the unnerved woman started foaming at the mouth and was whisked by helicopter to the Flowering Peachblossom Rest Home in Kyoto.

WHAT HAPPENED TO THE MALE SUBJECT?

His death certificate read: "electrocution by ejaculation." Poor Sayakawa; when he came, he went.

*"Attack! Attack! Attack!"

DOCTOR, WE HAVE HEARD THAT CIRCUMCISION IS AN ACCEPTABLE METHOD OF PENILE ALTERATION. WHAT EXACTLY IS IT?

The 11th Century alchemist, Merde de Mer, described it as a slice of life.

COULD YOU BE LESS PHILOSOPHICAL AND MORE TECHNICAL ABOUT IT?

Circumcision is a surgical procedure utilized to remove the prepuce (or foreskin) which covers the glans (or head) of the penis.

WHY?

Because the prepuce, if left where it is, may often deaden the exquisite sensation the head should be experiencing during sexual intercourse. In the wonderful world of sex, the term "deadhead" is no misnomer.
How lyrically was this concept put by the 13th Century poet-philosopher Omar Lingam!

> If you take away the foreskin,
> There's more fun for more skin.

To which I add a hearty right-on! And hard-on!

IN ADDITION TO THE ENHANCEMENT OF SEXUAL PLEASURE, IS THERE ANY OTHER

REASON FOR SUBMITTING TO CIRCUMCISION?

Most assuredly. In the uncircumcised penises of gentiles there lurk between the foreskin and the glans certain glands which exude a malodorous type of cheese called *smegma,* which will never win a blue ribbon from the Wisconsin Dairy Institute. In addition to its general unsavoriness, during the process of ejaculation smegma often outraces semen to the ovum, is fertilized, and the doleful consequence can be a woman who in nine months gives birth to a squirming bundle of gorgonzola.

But on circumcised Jewish penises there are glands which produce a pleasingly mild and flavorful substance, somewhat akin to a superior yogurt or sour cream, which is called *smetana,* a powerful enticement to any female. So one can perceive that, all religious considerations aside, in bed it's no joy to be a goy. Circumcision, like the all-new Plymouth, makes it.

WHO PERFORMS THIS SURGICAL PROCEDURE?

It can be done either by some young intern in a hospital ward or by a man steeped in Jewish ritual who is known as a *mohel,* which rhymes with *toil,* and that means there's trouble, big trouble in River City.

WHICH WOULD YOU CHOOSE?

The mohel—hands down.

WHY?

Taking your child to the hospital for this operation can be a stultifying experience. You sit in the waiting room leafing through the hospital's yellowing magazines (and, say, wasn't that a shame about the Titanic?) until the intern saunters over, muttering incoherent fragments through his boozy breath, although you do catch the word "malpractice" now and then. To him circumcision is all cut and dried and he is apt to perform it in a lackadaisical fashion. After all, it's no skin off *his* nose.

But circumcision is the mohel's art form and he approaches it with dignity. First of all, he comes to your house clad in a formal coat symbolic of his calling —a cutaway—whistling the time-honored march, "Pomp and Circumcision." Secondly, he brings a bottle of excellent Mogen David wine, some fluffy spongecake and a fund of rollicking jokes and anecdotes guaranteed to keep the parents and the infant howling, even during the surgery. He may also bring a book of Hadassah raffle tickets. (Indeed, while the tot is losing, his parents could be winning.) As he winds up his chore, he croons a comforting lullaby:

> Bye, bye, baby, I snipped away your bunting,
> For which you'll be grateful when broads you
>   are hunting.

WE AGREE WITH YOU, DOCTOR. THE MOHEL IS OUR CHOICE TOO. ARE THERE ANY OTHER METHODS OF CIRCUMCISION?

I did run across an unorthodox type of circumcision, the case of A.H., a frustrated young man unable to connect with a female. On a fateful night, he slid his penis across the centerfold of *Playboy* magazine, the slickness of the high-quality paper stock and the pythonish curves of Miss July contributing to a sturdy erection. But just when the matter was coming to a head, he hit a half-opened staple and became an instantaneous member of the International Zionist Conspiracy.

DID HE ADVISE PLAYBOY OF ITS INDIRECT RESPONSIBILITY FOR HIS PENILE MUTATION?

I told him not to. They're a rather uninspired bunch in Chicago, and if they'd told Hefner he would have botched up the ceremonial aspect, bringing Christian Brothers wine not Mogen David, Hostess Twinkies instead of spongecake, and instead of regaling the young man with hearty, knee-slapping jokes he would have read aloud from his yawn-provoking *Playboy* Philosophy. Despite his alleged bigtown sophistication, Hefner remains at heart a rurally oriented Methodist who believes the penis is nothing more than an undeveloped third leg.

IS CIRCUMCISION LIMITED TO MEN?

No. The Kikuyu tribe of East Africa used to remove the clitoris, the female mini-version of the penis, to insure the wife's fidelity whilst the husband was away chasing wildebeest or hartbeeste or just some beeste he met at a local bar. But the Kikuyu women of today, all of whom have read their Robert Ruark, won't permit this clitoral mutilation any more. "Nothing doing, my husband," they will say. "Not unless you replace it with 'Something of Value.'"

DOCTOR, YOU'VE TOLD US MUCH VALUABLE INFORMATION ABOUT THE PENIS, BUT WHAT ARE THE OTHER COMPONENT PARTS OF THE MALE ORGAN?

Certainly I would be remiss if I did not say something concerning the round structures which reside inside the scrotum (fleshy pouch) dangling beneath the penis. These are called testicles in the prepubertal years, but when the male reached a stage in his development in which he is capable of fatherhood we change the term slightly.

WHAT ARE THEY CALLED AT THAT STAGE?

Popsicles.

HOW MANY TESTICLES DOES A MAN HAVE?

Generally, two. Pawnbrokers have three.

ARE THERE MEN WHO DON'T HAVE ANY TESTICLES?

Yes. They are known as eunuchs.

WHAT IS THE DERIVATION OF THAT WORD?

In ancient days Middle Eastern caliphs (lords) owned large collections of lissome maidens known as harems. To insure that these women would not bestow their favors upon commoners while they were away, the caliphs stationed behind the harem doors guards whose testicles had been castrated (cut off) so that their own sexual desires would be stifled. Such a procedure naturally made the guards a mean bunch and when a hot-blooded swain would pound at the door demanding admittance he invariably would be met by a custodian brandishing a scimitar who snarled: "You knock, buddy? You knock?" From that day on these guards were given the derisive name "you-knock," which later was altered by the Greeks to "eunuch."

Another renowned group of eunuchs were the boy sopranos of the Middle Ages, who were castrated so that their high-pitched voices might never deepen. Historians of the period tell us that one of the most poignant moments of the service occurred when the choirboy-castrates chanted over and over in their sweetly sad way the haunting Latin air *Meae Nuces Sunt Perditae . . . Meae Nuces Sunt Perditae* (My Nuts Are Gone . . . My Nuts Are Gone. . . .)

WHAT ELSE DO THE TESTICLES DO?

They function as the sperm bank of the penis, but like any other bank they can't stand too many withdrawals or the male may lose his rate of interest and be forced into romantic bankruptcy.

ARE THERE ANY OTHER SIGNIFICANT PENILE PARTS WORTH MENTIONING?

I would say that the sensitive ring encircling the penis, the Corona—in Cuban men with cigar-shaped penises, the Corona Corona—is a vital part of a male's sexual enjoyment. This has been long known to women as the area capable of instant excitation, and as they stimulate the Corona either manually or orally they sing the jolly bit of erotic doggerel, "Ring Around the Penis! . . . Ring Around the Penis!"

HOW CAN THEY SING TO IT IF THEY ARE STIMULATING IT ORALLY?

Well, perhaps they can't articulate the lyrics in a meaningful way, but there's nothing to bar them from some perfectly thrilling humming.

CHAPTER FOUR

THE FEMALE: THE DICK CAVITY SHOW

DOCTOR WEINSTEIN, WHAT IS THE VAGINA?

A few years ago while vacationing in Colorado I made the acquaintance of Ranger Joe Ovid of the United States Forestry Service, and as we stood on the lip of a 1,500-foot cliff—Joe drinking in the beauty of the terrain, I a quart of Ripple Wine—his usually stern and rugged features became mistily contemplative.

"You know, Doc," he said, "I've been out here in the Golden West all my life and marveled at the ineffable handiwork of Nature, her sculptures and contours, but I would still have to conclude that, to me, the vagina is *the* Grand Canyon, *the* Great Divide."

A trifle miffed that he, a lowly civil servant, should fashion better vaginal metaphors than I, a superlative sexual expert, I pushed Ranger Joe over the side, and before he disappeared into the raging foam of the Colorado River I had already finished the Ripple Wine and forged an insurance policy making me his sole beneficiary. But let us desist from rhapsody to put the topic in a scientific framework. The vagina is the female organ for—

DOCTOR, PARDON THE INTERRUPTION, BUT YOU'VE JUST ADMITTED TO THE COLD-BLOODED MURDER OF A FINE HUMAN BEING JUST BECAUSE HE OUT-METAPHORED YOU. AREN'T YOU ASHAMED OF THIS GLARING FLAW IN YOUR MORAL MAKE-UP? HAVE YOU NO APOLOGY FOR THIS INDEFENSIBLE ACT?

The vagina is the female organ for sexual pleasure, located, like its penile playmate, in the pelvic triangle between the thighs. Pythagoras, the renowned Greek philosopher-mathematician, was once heard to say to a pupil, "Pliny, my boy, if you have to bisect a triangle, that's the one." And a Broadway musical comedy lyricist surely spoke for all men when he penned the title, "There's a Place for Us."

I personally have been an enthusiastic supporter of the vagina for many years and would like to see its story told with passion and vigor on the silver screen. To that purpose I am working on a scenario which I feel would be four-letter perfect for Elliott Gould and Donald Sutherland, who cavorted in the widely successful film *Mobile Army Surgical Hospital* (or *MASH*). Mine has the tentative title *Girls' Alluring Sexual Haven.*

IS THE VAGINA KNOWN BY ANY OTHER NAMES?

Yes, there are quite a few slang terms for the organ. Bakers and chefs, taking note of the vagina's fiery interior, have dubbed it the "oven for lovin'." Speleologists know it as the "cave of caves." One of the most common terms derives from the Latin name for the female genitalia, *cunnus,* which refers to its wedge-like shape. Ergo, men will often tell each other they're out looking for "some wedge." And professional football players, who have a terminology all their own, may say, "Let's go out and pick up a little punt."

One of the lesser known names for the vagina is the "mouth o' the south" or "southmouth" because it possesses some of the characteristics of its northern anatomical neighbor: lips, a beard and a moustache. But unlike the upper orifice it smiles vertically.

DOES THE "SOUTHMOUTH" (VAGINA) HAVE TEETH INSIDE LIKE THE PRIMARY MOUTH?

No. That's one of the old frightening legends that should have been dispelled a long time ago. Any male who has ever been inside the vagina knows it has no teeth; but it does have the most delightful gums.

AS YOU DID SO APTLY FOR THE PENIS, PLEASE DESCRIBE THE COMPONENT PARTS OF THE VAGINA. FIRST, WHAT IS THE VULVA?

The Vulva is the female counterpart of the Volvo. In hedonistic, sexually liberated Sweden where Vulvas are subjected to constant pounding, more than 90 per cent of them are still operative even after eleven or more years. One of the signs of a Vulva that has been in heavy use is a presence of a cheese-like substance that exudes from a gland.

OH, YES. YOU TOLD US ABOUT THAT CHEESY MATERIAL IN A PREVIOUS CHAPTER. SMEGMA, ISN'T IT?

No. In the female we call it Vulveeta. In this business you have to know your Kraft!

The area of the Vulva also includes two sets of moist lips: the outer, larger ones, the Labia Majora (Major Lips), and the inner, smaller pair, the Labia Minora (Minor Lips). With the major and minor melding so well during intercourse, anyone who tries to tell you there's no harmony in sex just doesn't know music.

Those labias, incidentally, prompted a traveling salesman from Muncie, Indiana, who was suspicious of his wife's perfidious propensities, to originate the saying, "Button your lips."

WHAT IS THE HYMEN?

It is a thin, penetrable membrane inside the vagina which, if unbroken, is supposed to signify a woman's virginity. We believe the hymen got its curious name from the fact that recent scientific examinations show it contains the vestigial remains of a larynx or voice-box. In those ancient days when it could talk, it supposedly whispered to passersby out of the side of its labial lips a provocative, "Hi, men!" Hence, the name.

SPEAKING OF VIRGINITY, WOMEN HAVE OFTTIMES GIVEN THEIR MEN SOME MIGHTY

FAR-FETCHED EXCUSES FOR ITS ABSENCE. FOR INSTANCE, CAN THE HYMEN BE BROKEN BY SLIDING DOWN A POLE?

Yes, or a Russian or a Bulgar or a Serb or a Croat. Any Slav will do.

DOCTOR, UP TO THIS POINT YOUR ANSWERS HAVE BEEN THE EPITOME OF HIGH-MINDEDNESS. AREN'T YOU THE LEAST BIT ABASHED TO HAVE PULLED OUT THIS HOARY WHEEZE?

I can't help it. I pulled it out of a wheezy hoar.

Getting back to virginity, though, an even more implausible fabrication for the rupture of the hymen is the old bedroom confession: "Oh, Bertram, my precious, believe me there has never been a man before you. It was broken on the seat of a bicycle." From the frequency with which this claim is made one would assume that the prime violator of womankind is that moustache-twirling old Don Juan, the Schwinn bicycle, and that the true slogan should be "in like *Schwinn*."

A BRILLIANT PUN, DOCTOR, AND THAT RESTORES OUR FAITH IN YOU. NOW, WHAT IS THE CLITORIS?

Ah, now we've come to the nitty-gritty of the female —or, if you prefer, the nitty-clitty. The clitoris is a tiny, cylindrically shaped body about an inch and a half in length situated at the top of the Vulva (by the by, wouldn't that be a stunning name for a San Francisco restaurant: the Top of the Vulva?) which, when stimulated by the penis, tongue or finger (and by the bye, wouldn't that be a stunning name for a rock group: Penis, Tongue & Finger?) is capable of the most exquisite sexual sensations. When this organ —the boom-boom of the broad, the seat of the heat, the button for ruttin'—is triggered into this awesome boiling phase, which we call a "clit fit," it can be analogous to an H-Bomb going off, in our terms, a nooky lear explosion.

The word "clitoris" comes from the Greek and means "key" (one of the few times, incidentally, that the Greeks have ever been known to be forward-looking). It truly is the key to a woman's happiness, and we all know what sort of man is qualified to make a key stir.

LET'S SEE. A MAN ADEPT WITH KEYS. WOULD THAT BE A LOCKSMITH?

That's close enough.

It should be noted that the vagina, which if seen in a cross-section diagram appears to have the shape of the letter H, (remember the pattern we learned on our old stick-shift automobile?), is altered dramatically during this clitoral rampage into a sort of internal cylinder. So the man who still recalls the correct way to shift gears will be in the driver's seat for a long time, and the hell with Greyhound or Hertz.

DOCTOR, WHEN THE FEMALE HAS AN ORGASM DOES SHE EJACULATE LIKE THE MALE?

No. As far as we are able to determine, there is no external gush of semen. But we certainly can deduce from the little things she does at the peak of her performance that she has achieved a satisfactory orgasm. She may, at that magical moment, break the world's record for pole vaulting. She may do a hundred cartwheels. She may sing all the parts of the Hallelujah Chorus from Handel's *Messiah*. She may bestow prolonged, gleeful applause upon her lover, by smashing together both her hands and her labial lips.

Too, a clear sign of a woman satisfied is the phenomenon we call the "orgasmic flush," the sudden blossoming of roseate blotches which begins on her neck and moves in horizontal fashion across her breasts, stomach and navel, arranging itself into the words: "I love you . . . I love you . . . I love you . . . !"

WHAT IF THE WOMAN IS OF ORIENTAL LINEAGE?

Then the blotches will run up and down, but still they will spell: "I love you . . . I love you . . . I love you . . . !"

LET'S DEVIATE FOR A MOMENT. SINCE YOU MENTIONED ORIENTAL WOMEN, TELL

US: ARE THEY REALLY BUILT DIFFERENTLY AS THE LEGEND WOULD HAVE IT?

Of course. The old saying, "Ever since I had an affair with Susie Wong, I got a new slant on women" is a verity. A Caucasian male may find this sexual difference appealing, but Oriental men, who are also built on a slant, don't notice it at all.

GETTING BACK TO THE VAGINA YOU JUST DESCRIBED, IS THERE ANY CONDITION THAT COULD HAVE ROBBED IT OF ITS PLEASURE?

I intend to deal with the problems of impotence and dysfunction in the female genitalia in a subsequent chapter. However, there is one problem that could have made the female in my illustration a thoroughly miserable creature and that is the physiological one called "hyperacidity." Sometimes too much acid builds up in the vagina for various reasons, but the cure is fairly simple.

HOW CAN YOU STOP HYPERACIDITY IN THE VAGINA?

By dropping in one or two Rolaid tablets. That should quickly ease the condition. Yet extreme caution should be taken not to insert too many Rolaids or a terrible tragedy might ensue.

WHAT COULD HAPPEN?

As you know from watching this product's long-running television commercials, Rolaids consumes forty-seven times its own weight. If an excessive amount is introduced, it could cause the disappearance of the vagina and any hapless penis that happens to be in it.

Another physiological handicap is the too-tight vagina, which we refer to in clinical terminology as the organ-grinder or nutcracker. The cure for this is also within current medical competence. The constricted organ can either be widened by surgery or a pin-sized charge of plastique explosive.

CAN VAGINAS ACCOMMODATE ANY SIZE PENIS?

Yes. The normal vagina is a flexible mechanism that can handle just about anything that comes its way. I did say, however, that most women do prefer to receive the larger penis, as is clearly borne out by the case of one of my patients, the infamous British strumpet, Katrina Rice-Mandy.

WHAT IS A STRUMPET?

The female personification of a trumpet; in other words, a hooker with a magnificently developed *embouchure* (lip function). Miss Rice-Mandy began her stirring strumpet solos at the age of sixteen when, on a particularly swinging session with Harry James's big band, she blew out her Cherry-Biri-Bin. As is well known, she became the center of a raging scandal in

London after it was learned she was introducing foreign objects into her vagina, namely, Russian embassy spies. "It beats pencils, combs and mop handles," she told the press.

Then she moved into some rather exalted circles and, in addition to bedding with the Russians, took on several Members of the British Parliament. When I asked her which group of men she preferred, she said the latter.

WHY?

As she so charmingly put it, "Parliament gives you that extra quarter of an inch."

GOOD THINKING ON HER PART. TO CONTINUE: WE REALIZE NOW THAT THE VAGINA CAN SERVICE JUST ABOUT ANY SIZE PENIS, BUT HOW BIG IS IT ACTUALLY?

The vagina is usually no bigger than four to five inches in its non-sexual state, being somewhat like a collapsed balloon. Fortunately, there must be millions and millions of circus fans on this earth, for there is no shortage of individuals willing to blow it up.

DOES THE PENIS EVER CAUSE THE VAGINA PAIN?

Only if the penis doesn't function, but that pain, of course, is psychological. Physiologically speaking, it is very rare for the vagina to feel pain, no matter how large and demanding the penis, because, in addition to being expandable, it has a kind of self-lubricating mechanism built in. Those half-baked sexual "experts" I've been at odds with used to believe this lubrication was caused by the structures on either side of the lower vagina called Bartholin's Glands, but I have disproved this beyond doubt.

HOW?

I had the common sense to place—at great expense to myself, may I add—a long-distance call to Bartholin. He said no, his glands have nothing whatsoever to do with it, and I took him at his words, fine gentleman that he is.

The lubrication *is* performed by the walls of the vagina themselves, which secrete a slippery sweat-like substance making the penis feel it's on the niftiest bobsled run in creation. If a man asks a woman if she can perform sexually and she says, "No sweat," he must not take that as a favorable omen.

HOW LONG DOES THIS SELF-LUBRICATING PROCESS LAST?

Smoothly (one couldn't say roughly in this instance) for about 2,000 episodes of sexual intercourse. When it goes beyond that figure, the vagina should be taken to a good Swedish doctor and replaced. On the male the Corona, or ring around the penile head, may also be worn down badly at this stage. A simple "ring job" is called for in his case.

Next stop: sexual intercourse, the real national pastime, which we usher in with the traditional cry, "Play balls!"

CHAPTER FIVE

SEXUAL INTERCOURSE: A SERMON ON THE MOUNTING

DOCTOR, WHAT IS SEXUAL INTERCOURSE?

Simply stated, sexual intercourse is a coupling of physical entities, an exciting form of body contact?

BUT, DOCTOR, AREN'T THE BOXCARS ON A FREIGHT TRAIN, WHICH CERTAINLY COULD BE DESCRIBED AS PHYSICAL ENTITIES, ALSO INVOLVED IN AN ACTIVITY CALLED "COUPLING"? AND AREN'T FOOTBALL, BASKETBALL, WRESTLING, LACROSSE, HOCKEY AND THE LIKE ALSO KINDS OF EXCITING BODY CONTACT?

You may have a point there. Perhaps my definition was a trifle vague, so let's start afresh. Sexual intercourse is a highly specialized coupling bringing together two or more *non-ferrous** and *non-boxcar-shaped*** entities in a vastly superior brand of physical

---

* In truth, there is a small portion of iron in human organisms, but happily not enough to rust the sexual organs.
** In truth, though humans are not shaped like rectangles, some do make love like squares.

contact sport containing less pain and more pleasure than the usual contact sports and which does not require considerable outlays for uniforms, equipment, marching bands, officials, and stadium or fieldhouse rentals.

That, I think, should bring the matter into sharper focus. By the way, there actually may be some form of sexual expression among those boxcars you cited. Think now; have you ever strolled through a freight yard and noticed signs on some of the boxcars that warn, "DO NOT HUMP"? This may just be some obscure slang whose meaning is known only to railroad personnel, but can we be sure that it is not an erotic reference? After all, when boxcars are on the roll there's some pretty wild squealing and colliding going on.

Of course, an individual's ethnic or educational conditioning may also determine his outlook on sexual intercourse. The Japanese, for example, consider it to be the consummate form of massage wherein both the masseuse and massagee get rubbed. A Marxist may feel it's an activity designed by Wall Street solely to keep people's minds off the class struggle. And so forth.

WHAT IS YOUR PERSONAL POSITION ON SEX?

I'm afraid I couldn't delineate my position on sex without resorting to such complicated terms as "hot Santa Ana winds," "I-formation," "show and tell," "vertical takeoff," "chewy caramel centers," "front end alignment," etc.

NO, DOCTOR, WE DIDN'T MEAN TO PRY INTO YOUR PERSONAL, OBVIOUSLY INTIMATE, BEDROOM TECHNIQUES. WE WANTED TO KNOW, HOW DO YOU FEEL ABOUT SEXUAL INTERCOURSE PHILOSOPHICALLY?

Oh, I see. And it's a good thing I was shunted from this line of thought because I was just about to describe the "tusk and musk at dusk" arrangement which leads automatically to the "knotted string and the playground swing" technique, both of which should only be practiced by the higher life forms, porpoises and cybernauts.

If you ask me how I view sex in a philosophical way I would say I have always thought it was a desirable activity and here is my reasoning, which I'm sure you will find unassailable:

If the Divine Intelligence who created us all had intended sex to be a frightening, repellent affair, then the sexual organs would not fuse in an ambience of such sublime, succulent slipperiness. Imagine, if you will, a penis driving into a vagina only to discover its interior houses a nest of scorpions or a set of revolving lawnmower blades or, conversely, a vagina forced to receive a penis studded from glans to testicles with cockleburrs and spiny thorns. But such is not the case. The organs feel marvelous in concert (no matter what composer is being featured), which leads me to believe that sex is healthy, natural and proper.

YOU MENTIONED THE WORD "HEALTHY." CAN SEXUAL INTERCOURSE ADVANCE THE CAUSE OF GOOD HEALTH, FOR EXAMPLE,

BY TAKING AWAY PIMPLES AS THE OLD STORY GOES?

Whenever this question is posed, I invariably hear a chorus of snickers (odd really . . . it's overindulgence with Snickers and other candy products that may cause pimples in the first place!), but then I swiftly counter with the case history of Rusty, and that quashes the scoffers. (By the bye, wouldn't that be a marvelous name for a daytime television quiz game? "Hi! I'm Wink Martindale and it's time to play—'Quash the Scoffers!'").

On the day that 16-year-old, redheaded Mark "Rusty" Twain, a likeable stringbean from Hannibal, Missouri, was brought to me by his parents, he was in a bad way, epidermis-wise. His adorable freckles were fighting for their very right to exist on a face that appeared to be a loathsome lunar crater, so marred was it by angry acne clusters, pillars of pustules, an Andean chain of carbuncles and boils, plus other blemishes too revolting to mention.

After quizzing Rusty in private, I shrewdly deduced that his facial nightmare was due in the main to the stagnating, fettered hormones in his system. I promptly prescribed a program of controlled sexual relations with a pixieish baton twirler, Samantha Sigafoos, who had been accorded the title of "Miss Go All The Way" at the junior prom by her class's enthusiastic male members (and *their* enthusiastic male members). Inducing her to cooperate in the experiment was a simple matter of promising to star her in a skin flick called "Mondo Batono Twirlero," currently packing them in at the Pussycat Theater in Santa Monica as part of a triple bill including "Born To Be Bitten" and "Stomp Me If You Love Me."

I saw in the annual Hannibal High Harvest Hayride an opportune occasion for the launching of the experiment. As the mules loped along at a slow clip-clop the kids trilled the autumnal hymn "Bringing in the Sheaves," Rusty and Samantha working on their own version, "Swinging in the Sheaves." The following afternoon an elated Rusty bounded into my clinic pointing to the left side of his face. "Look, doc, look!" A clump of the hideous blotches had vanished, leaving the field to winsome freckles.

"And, doc," he said shyly, looking down at his Thom McAn desert boots, "somethin' sorta popped outa me last night. I don't know what it was but it felt good and—"

"That's fine, Rusty, just fine. There's a long, technical explanation for what it was, but as far as your treatment is concerned let's just call it 'vanishing cream.'"

Relieved, he resumed the treatment and in the weeks that followed he and Samantha found many suitable occasions for stimulating his long dormant glands—parties, homework sessions together, the senior play, which fortunately that year was "Marat Sade," Saturday nights at the local passion pit, etc., and in six weeks Rusty's visage was Dorian Gray Before, completely devoid of the eruptions that had made his social life a horror.

"Well, Rusty," I smiled. "You can terminate the program now. You look like Every Boy, U.S.A., with that curling grin, red head and those adorable freckles. I wouldn't be surprised to see your face on the cover of Field & Stream one of these days."

To my amazement, he snapped: "Stop it, hell! I dig it so much that I intend to step it up to four times a day. Sam has moved out of her house and we're living together in a lean-to on old Judge Procol

Harum's farm." And he spun on his heels, walked out and I never saw him again.

WE'RE FASCINATED BY THIS CASE HISTORY. TELL US, WHATEVER HAPPENED TO YOUNG RUSTY?

Some weeks after he walked out on me, I received a letter from his parents:

Dear Dr. Weinstein,
We can never thank you enough for recommending the treatment that rid Rusty's face of its horrible colonies of blemishes. We realize that you warned him against continuance of this procedure once the condition had cleared up, so we can't find it in our hearts to condemn you for what transpired. Against your orders Rusty quadrupled his bouts of intercourse with Samantha until not only did the blemishes disappear, but also his adorable freckles, his ruddy All-American boy complexion and finally even the russet tresses that earned him his nickname. Rusty—now the kids call him Whitey—is today a complete albino, but he's a happy albino, so if he's happy, we're happy.

NOW THAT YOU'VE COMPLETED THE SAGA OF RUSTY, WE'RE HAPPY TOO. TO CONTINUE: WHAT ARE THE POSITIONS USED IN SEXUAL INTERCOURSE?

The most common is the face-to-face, man-atop-woman arrangement which the regulars down at the gym call "pushups with a partner." I have known portly, puffing men who have increased their pushup quotient from ten to 435 an hour after being introduced to this method, and I predict that the Y will witness a fantastic resurgence of popularity if it scraps losers like Beginning and Advanced Jogging from its exercise program and replaces them with this crowd pleaser.

Another name for the above mentioned technique is the "missionary position," this coined by South Sea Islanders observing how visiting missionaries made love. The general consensus among the islanders was expressed in a recent interview granted the *Tonga Times-Outrigger* newspaper by Goinawahinebehiney, the 120-year-old chieftain, who, recalling the early days of the missionary era, remarked, "If that was the only way those bleached-out, gold-toothed, psalm-shrieking holy rollers got it on, they had one hell of a nerve tampering with our blissful barbarian *shtik*." He also had a few ill-tempered comments about James Michener's novels, Seven Seas' Green Goddess salad dressing and Don Ho's nightclub act, none of which needs inclusion here.

ARE THERE ANY ADVANTAGES TO THE FACE-TO-FACE POSITION OF INTERCOURSE?

Well, an obvious one is that you can see the face of the person you are about to make love to, thus allowing for a last-minute change of mind.

It is also easier to kiss the lips of the love partner. A man practicing the rear entry procedure may traumatize the neck muscles severely in a foolish attempt to twist his head into an attitude permitting a full-mouth kiss. The most he can achieve is a corner of the mouth any way—and it may not be the better of the corners.

Loving face to face also permits the partners a full view of some of the more provocative, libido-igniting frontal body structures, i.e., flaring nostrils that reveal venous cartilage, interesting formations of dental tartar, the adam's apple abob in a sea of passion, the "love handles" quivering at the hips and the bellybutton, which, of course, should be vacuumed before intercourse by one of the smaller Hoover attachments to remove desire-deadening lint.

IS THE REAR ENTRY ATTACK A VALID ONE?

Yes, but only if the man is behind the behind. For obvious reasons woman-behind-man is a distressing waste of time and talent. All her vagina gets to abut is his butt or, worse, his coccyx, which, despite a pronunciation fraught with promise, is nothing more than a small triangular bone at the lower end of the spinal column not eminently noted for its capacity to thrill; his erect penis meanwhile is going nowhere, just poking at the air, and the air doesn't care.

DOCTOR, YOUR DESCRIPTIONS OFTTIMES ARE PURE POETRY. NOW THAT WE'VE DECIDED THAT THE MAN SHOULD BE BEHIND

THE WOMAN, WHAT ARE THE BENEFITS OF THIS METHOD?

Working from the rear a man is able to accomplish a few significant maneuvers: (A) Thus positioned, he can better stimulate his lover's clitoris, for it is more accessible to his finger than in the face-to-face setup. (One gentle rub of the nub and "the little boy in the boat" is off on the royal regatta to romance.) (B) He also can, as he whips in and out of the vagina, massage the navel, titillate the tits (or teatillate the teats, if you want to be consistent about it) or even, if he times his strokes, perform a Papp test. (C) And because his lips are directly behind her ears he can inflame her further by whispering the hot words of love.

YOU'VE VENTURED INTO A TOUCHY AREA HERE: PROFANITY. ISN'T IT CHEAPENING THE SACRED ACT OF LOVE TO EMPLOY THESE SPOKEN VULGARITIES?

If ever there was a time to cast aside the shackles of conventional behavior, it is during that Sealy Posturepedic bounce-in. For heaven's sake, let go! In every way . . . and that includes panting those taboo terms frowned upon and shunned by polite society. Here the two of you are, jaybird naked, so is this the time for puerile restraint? Gosh no! Tell her: "Oh, my darling, to think that my tumescent member is hovering in the vicinity of your introitus."

YOU'D SAY—THAT?

Yes, dammit, I would, I have and I intend to again. Go on, free yourself for once and for all. Say it! Liberate your mind!

INTROITUS, INTROITUS, INTROITUS! YOU'RE RIGHT. IT FEELS SIMPLY MARVY! WHAT NEXT SHOULD A MAN SAY?

"Oh, my jewel, never in my entire history of penile penetrations have I ever encountered vaginal walls exuding such thermal lubricity."

OH, DOCTOR. WE FEEL LIKE RUSHING INTO A COLD SHOWER! WHAT NEXT?

"My love slave, what well coordinated abductor muscles you own! What levators, what constrictor cunni, what fossa navicularis vulvae!"

WILL THIS EXCITE HER INTO USING SIMILAR RACY LANGUAGE?

Definitely. Since by nature women are more reticent than men about using sexual language, she may begin to respond in a timid fashion: "Your corpora cavernosa are pretty nice." But once the sweet starter fluid of love has been sprayed on the barbecue pit of her passion, there will be no stopping her. "Oh angel," she will breathe, "I adore your walnut-like prostate, the thumping of your scrotum, your pulsating pudendum, your liquid-bearing vas deferens. . . ." And the affair will rush onward to a thrilling climax, interrupted only when the lovers disengage from time to time to sprint to a medical dictionary for more wild, inflammatory sexual terms. Among the others guaranteed to keep that heat flowing from body to body are: Cowper's glands, mons veneris, urethal meatus, fourchette, epididymis, and my personal favorite, bulbospongiosum. Lovers who take special pains to memorize these terms will benefit themselves in two ways: (A) They will become superb bedmates; (B) They will find themselves winning a flock of Scrabble games.

WHAT ARE SOME OF THE OTHER POSITIONS OF INTERCOURSE?

Along with the man-atop-woman-face-to-face and the man-behind-woman, we have woman-atop-man-face-to-face, woman-sitting-atop-man (the so-called "hot squat"), man-and-woman-side-to-side, man-astride-side-to-side, woman-astride-side-to-side, the Greek cheek-to-cheek (the organs do not touch, but it is a fine preliminary bit of fun, permitting the lovers to bash each other's buttocks in a rollicking game of boomps-a-daisy) and the Continental. The latter should be performed with the man in full white tie and tails regalia, the woman in a 1930-ish puff-shouldered evening gown and in the background a high-spirited array of Busby Berkley-directed, leggy chorines to give it an added fillip.

Kent can s up to 55% on these

A Hallmark His and Hers Mini Hair Dryer
Completely portable. Tucks neatly into purse or briefcase. Blows hot air instantly. Thermostatically controlled. Long cord. In black or white.
Retail Value $10.95
Kent Price .... $ 4.68

B Hallmark Hi/Lo Wall and Desk Hi-Intensity Lamp
Thumb controlled hi-lo switch for brilliant pure white light to soft glow. Converts to night light. Full-flex telescoping arm. High-impact styrene. Swivels 360 degrees. In black or white.
Retail Price $6.95
Kent Price $3.75

You can get these fabulous premiums at big savings. Use the coupon to select the item(s) you wish to order. Send check or money order, along with two bottom flaps from any Kent Regular or Menthol package (King size or Deluxe 100's) for each premium ordered.

Regular Kings: 16 mg. "tar", 1.0 mg. nicotine;
Regular 100's: 19 mg. "tar", 1.2 mg. nicotine av. per cigarette, FTC Report Nov. '70.
Menthol Kings: 18 mg. "tar", 1.1 mg. nicotine;
Menthol 100's: 18 mg. "tar", 1.2 mg. nicotine; av. per cigarette by FTC method.

Now Kent Menthol comes in King size, too.

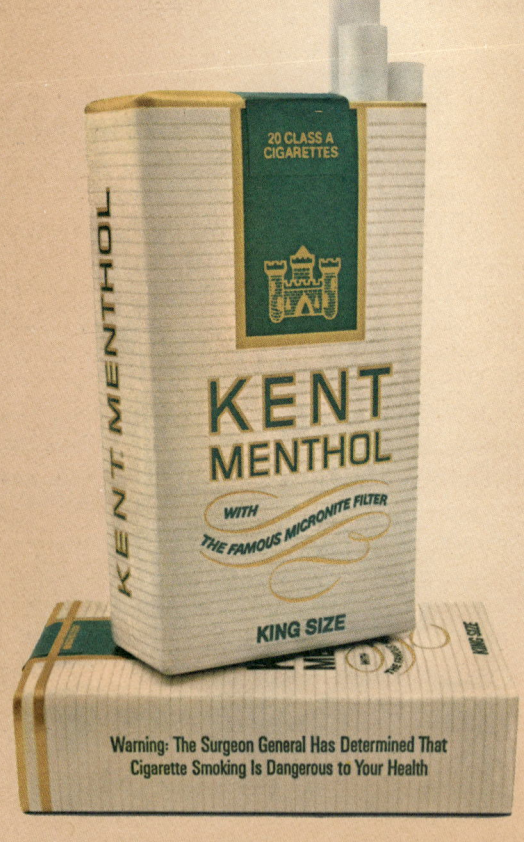

Warning: The Surgeon General Has Determined That Cigarette Smoking Is Dangerous to Your Health

Special premium values inside!

WILL THE PERUSAL OF THOSE ANCIENT FAR EASTERN SEX MANUALS GIVE US SOME INTERESTING VARIATIONS?

I assume you're referring to the Kama Kala, the Kama Sutra and the Kama Kazi.

WE'VE HEARD OF THE FIRST TWO, BUT WHAT IS THE KAMA KAZI?

It's the Japanese love manual, of fairly recent vintage, but I don't recommend it because it calls for the man to don goggles, a silken scarf and buckteeth, scream "Banzai!" and make love to a woman on the wing of a bomb-laden Zero diving into the side of an American aircraft carrier. It's strictly a one-shot affair, quite expensive (obtaining a Zero and a carrier may strain the average budget; even Neiman-Marcus doesn't carry these items in its catalogue) and not worth the effort.

The Kama Kala, although interesting from a scholar's point of view, need not concern us because it deals with sexual relationships between moss, yeasty molds and poison sumac. The Kama Sutra is another story.

Composed some six thousand years ago by L'hal L'luhyah, a sage of the Lesser Way, this venerable work was brought out last year in a newly revised, modernized edition by L'hal L'luhyah's youngest son, the pundit Pandit, a personal friend of this author. The Kama Sutra divides the sexes into various groupings, according to the size of their physical endowments and the depth of their passion. Men, for instance, are broken down into three main categories: the hare man, generally a short-penised, shy type; the bull man, an intermediate range individual; and the horse man, the obvious winner in any Derby. Women also are characterized in three ways: deer woman, mare woman and the superpotent elephant woman. L'hal L'luhyah himself once warned a hare man who had the temerity to fall in love with an elephant woman: "Don't do it. You're going in way over your head."

It also suggests certain offbeat routines for jaded appetites, but topnotch physical condition is mandatory before exploring them. Lovers who have spent the required number of hours doing the Royal Canadian Air Force exercises—I gave them up myself; I was damn tired of running up to Montreal every morning—probably possess the fitness to do the following:

First, they disrobe and luxuriate together in a sunken Roman bath filled with cobra's milk. During the loveplay, the man may stimulate his partner's yoni with a few squirts from a Water-Pik; she may reciprocate by running her fingertips gently yet firmly across his lingam until it elevates to the proper height, but if the lingam hisses and snaps at her pinkie, let her beware; the Bombay shipping firm may have neglected to cull the cobra from the milk. Shaking off the drops of milk—probably a glob or two of butter as well; after all, they've been churning around pretty vigorously in there—they emerge from the tub and rub each other with Turkish towels interwoven with strands of barbed wire to give the skin that healthy reddish tingle. The male sprays himself with Right Guard, then Left Guard, for he should leave no flank unprotected. The female, meanwhile, applies a thin layer of yak marrow to her pubic area, then retreats to the opposite side of the room to lie down, her legs splayed out invitingly to receive the booming thrust of his turgid lingam.

Driven to frenzy by the sight of her glistening, winking, pinkish treasure, he scales the curtains, grasps the sash, rocks back and forth to gain momentum, and with a wrenching cry of "hare krishna!" ("I adore your hairy krishna!" in the Hindi tongue) he hurtles toward her in a swashbuckling leap worthy of Douglas Fairbanks, Sr. Or Sammy Davis, Jr. If he connects, the result will be a sensation of indescribable ecstasy.

WHAT IF HE DOESN'T CONNECT?

Then he rams six inches into the television set and climaxes in Dinah's Place. Or worse, McHale's Navy.

ALBEIT EXCITING, THIS ROUTINE SEEMS TOO STRENUOUS FOR MOST PEOPLE. COULD YOU RECOMMEND ONE LESS TAXING AND PERILOUS FOR AVERAGE FOLKS?

I suppose there are those who might consider plucking a few glass shards from the front of a Magnavox out of their crotches an irritant, so let me offer an alternate routine, less athletic, to be sure, but just as satisfying to the senses. Presuming all the preliminary procedures have been duly performed—and these include checking into a disreputable hotel on the wrong side of town under assumed names (even if married) to evoke that glorious feeling of shame and degradation, toasting one another with a cheap wine favored by derelicts, throwing a rope of knotted bedsheets out the window as a potential hurry-up escape route (if you're on the ground floor do it anyway; it adds to the excitement), etc.—the affair should begin with the lovers verbalizing their most intimate fantasies.

AREN'T THESE FANTASIES A BIT ON THE CHILDISH SIDE?

Perhaps so, but if they provide that enticing slice of forbidden fruit, then I say go ahead and conjure up the bizarrest fantasies imaginable. (NOTE: As a confirmed heterosexual,* however, I do not counsel the literal fantasizing about forbidden fruit.)

DO YOU PERSONALLY INDULGE IN THESE FANTASIES?

Quite often. My love partner and I have concocted scores of them, and they heighten the enjoyment in a most delightful way. In a recent enactment, she was the lovely, virginal Princess Snow White, harboring a secret desire to be ravished by all of the Seven Dwarfs at once—a severe strain on my histrionic talent. For a while it was a hectic business switching in and out of six different voices and seven different faces and attitudes, and indeed, toward the end my Dopey began to droop, but fortunately my Doc and Grumpy got it altogether with a "Heigh-Ho, Heigh-Ho" that blew the roof off the dwarf's cottage.

Sometimes she, the strong-willed, spoiled-rotten Scarlet O' Tara, mistress of Hara, commands me,

---

* Confirmed by the UPI, AP and Reuters.

Rhett Butler, to sweep her into my brawny arms and charge up a long, winding staircase to the boudoir, sneering, "By God, Scarlett, there'll only be one man in your bed tonight and it won't be that dandified peacock Ashley Wilkes!" (We had to jettison this playlet the day my Weight Watchers report came back negative and it was back to the goddam bean sprouts.) We've also freaked out in "The Hun and the Nun" (she is dewy-eyed Sister Clotilde cowering before me, the slavering Atilla), "The Wino and the Rhino" (gin-guzzling Contessa Madeline DeRochemont, weary of the inept lovemaking of her paramour, Sir Derek Pisherkeh-Throgg, thrashes her restless, naked body in her tent on a sultry Congo night; I, Taga, a nightmarish, four-thousand-pound quadruped, lumber in thunderously; she spots me, whispers, "Oh, you're so . . . so horny"; she gets the African thirst, pours a case of Simba over my leathery carcass and we make it), and an up-to-date fantasy in which she, portraying Broadway Josephine Namath, first Women's Lib member to crack the National Football League, hungers to be violated by a proud and domineering superman, whom I play. (This one didn't work well until I put in three Monday nights at the TV mastering my characterization of Howard Cosell.)

HAVING BEEN STIRRED BY THESE VIVID FANTASIES, WHAT'S NEXT ON YOUR AMOROUS AGENDA FOR THIS COUPLE?

They move on to the foreplay phase, which I call Preorgasmic Exploration Time (PET), involving the gratification of the five senses: seeing, smelling, touching, hearing and tasting. To excite the first, I would suggest at this point undressing, but not the precipitate, helter-skelter flinging about of clothes à la a pair of overheated, callow teenagers. Mature undressing should be langorous, deliberate, at a snail's pace. (My clinic can furnish for a modest rental fee an excellent film demonstrating a snail undressing that runs only nine thousand minutes and is worth emulating. I know of a woman who did, and made such a project out of slow, seductive disrobing that her lover had to pay three days' rent to the motel and shave six times before the act was consummated.)

As his partner's delicious flesh is revealed to him . . . inch by inch, pore by pore* . . . the man's hands knot into trembling balls, his balls into trembling hands, his throat tightens, for there in front of his eyes is that most pleasing of all artistic masterworks, the S-curve of a woman's body.** He responds, slowly peels off his Stud of the Loom*** underwear, and her hands knot into trembling balls, her breasts heave and her eyes feast upon his manly barrel chest. (If he chooses to remove the barrel, so much the better.) When his throat begins to heave and her chest tightens, they have arrived at that state of visual bliss. If I may be forgiven a personal reminiscence, my first visual experience was even profounder. Upon seeing my love partner's unclothed form, my eyes popped out, when she saw my nakedness her eyes popped

---

* At this stage, ladies, pore it on!
** A study I made for the Council for Rigid Automobile Safety on Highways (CRASH) proves conclusively that more accidents occur on roads with S-curves. A man motors on one, thinks he is traversing a woman's body, turns dreamy and inattentive and—whomp!—he's splattered all over the front counter of Howard Johnson's.
*** I know it's Fruit of the Loom, but I've made my position on this quite clear.

out, and we spent our first tryst on our hands and knees searching for each other's eyes. Fortunately, mine were green and easier to spot in the dim light.

SMELLING IS THE SECOND SENSE ON YOUR PREORGASMIC EXPLORATION TIME (PET) CHECKLIST, BUT FRANKLY, DOCTOR, ISN'T IT... VULGAR?

Smelling is vulgar? Rank nonsense! If we can go into rhapsodies over the fragrance of a flower that was nurtured in compost or the warm scent of a beloved, lop-eared puppydog that's been heaven only knows where, then why be hesitant about sniffing the human body? Of course, we naturally assume that our lovers, prior to close contact, have showered vigorously out of respect for each other's susceptibilities ("a dirty mind in a clean body" is my axiom) with Axiom, an Arthur Godfrey-approved biodegradable cleansing agent out of respect to the environment. If they have, then let their olfactory bulbs romp to their noses' content. By golly, I sure as shootin' wouldn't mind a little Senta (Scent O') Berger!

ANOTHER DAZZLING PUN, DOCTOR. NOW, HOW ABOUT TOUCHING?

That's PET's third sense and it calls for the sly roaming of the fingers over mound and curve and into crack and crevice. (By the bye, wouldn't that be a smashing lead article for *The National Geographic*: "Over Mound and Curve and Into Crack and Crevice"?) It is a fact that each opening in the body or orifice*—we refer here to the nose, ears, mouth, vagina, anus and bellybutton—contains at its entrance a network of sensitive nerve-endings which when probed oh so gently experience a high degree of excitation. Hence, the lover who is able to stimulate with his fingertips *all these orifices at the same time* will receive (A) his partner's everlasting gratitude for being such a "soft touch" and (B) a telegram from me offering to be this individual's show business representative, for anyone who can pull off this trick must have an extra arm or fingers tucked away somewhere, and Ed Sullivan would go positively bananas for the chance to exhibit these novelties on television.

If all the procedures I have outlined thus far have been adhered to with slavish fidelity, then the gratification of our fourth sense, hearing, is logically in full swing. By now the lovers are serenading each other with a cacophony of carnal cries and a volley of vowels that ripple the jowls and bestir the bowels: amorous aaaaahs ... erotic eeeeehs ... open-throated ooooohs ... unrestrained ummmmmms ... and things are so hot and heavy at this point that even a funky "o-y-y-y!" may escape through quivering lips, but who cares?

AND THAT BRINGS US TO THE FIFTH SENSE, TASTING, ONE THAT MAY OFFEND DEEPLY THOSE OF YOUR READERS WHO

---

* Sample usage: A woman who has just been made love to by one man and is being solicited by a second may say: "I already gave at the orifice."

ARE STILL IMPRISONED BY THAT RESTRICTIVE PURITAN TRADITION. WHAT DO YOU FEEL ABOUT ORAL SEX?

I'm all for it—as long as it's in good taste. But we are getting ahead of ourselves, so let's wait until ourselves catches up. First we ought to discuss the initial phase of oral sex which is kissing?

WHAT IS KISSING?

Mouth-to-mouth resuscitation between two people, neither of whom is anywhere near water nor in danger of drowning.

A CLEAR DEFINITION. NOW, WHAT IS THE "SOUL KISS"?

When two black lovers bring their tongues together. Similar contact between two South Koreans is labeled the "Seoul kiss," between two members of the Hebraic heritage a "Sol kiss," two Eskimos a "Seal kiss." And so forth.

The secondary phase is oral-genital and oral-anal and, if practiced with evangelical fervor in a large tent, oral-roberts.

In connection with oralism one should understand the meaning of the suffix, *lingus,* which is the Latin word for "tongue." Thus we have a practice featuring the tongue inserted into the auditory orifice, earilingus, sometimes known as "playing it by ear."

Exciting as earilingus is, it can be doubly so if the

individual doing the licking (henceforth to be designated the licker) also blows jets of hot air into the ear of the person he is stimulating (the lickee). Upon occasions excessive amounts of interior material—or "wax buildup"—may dull the lickee's enjoyment, but a few drops of Lemon Pledge on the tip of the licker's tongue quickly unclog the passageway and also give the ear a glossy attractiveness.

Other examples of oral sex are nipplingus (eating the nipple), bubbilingus (eating the entire breast), toeilingus (eating the toe), anklingus (the ankle), browilingus (the brow), cunnilingus (the female genitalia), penilingus (the male genitalia, also called fellatio), anilingus (the anus) and dingilingus.

WHAT IS DINGILINGUS?

The desire in a male to eat the Avon Lady. (The Fuller Brush man in females.) This form gets its name from the characteristic sound of the door chimes.

The most prevalent type of oralism is simultaneous cunnilingus-fellatio, referred to in slang, because of the positioning of the practitioners' bodies, as "sixty-nine." The French call it soixante-neuf (sixty-nine), the Spanish sesenta y neuve (sixty-nine), the Germans neun und sechzig (sixty-nine).

ORAL SEX SEEMS SUCH A SOPHISTICATED PRACTICE. ARE WE CORRECT IN ASSUMING

THAT AMONG THE MAMMALS ONLY MAN DOES IT?

You can say that in a dog-eat-dog world?

WE'D FORGOTTEN THAT. DOCTOR, IS ORAL SEX INCREASING IN POPULARITY?

Yes, and I think its vogue is due in no small measure to television, which has placed emphasis upon the mouth as the primary receptacle for the genitals. Those tight camera shots on an Ultra-Brite toothpaste mouth blowing lipsticked kisses every which way and squealing "Wheeeee . . . sex appeal!", the Lavoris mouth and its "pucker power" (substitute another consonant for the "p" in the "pucker" and you'll get their drift), the Certs mouth, the Scope mouth, etc., all seem to lead to an ineluctable conclusion: If the mouth is that groovy, why bother hitting below the belt?

HOW CAN THE SPOTLIGHT BE PUT BACK UPON THE GENITALS AS THE PRIMARY COURCE OF PLEASURE IN SEX?

By literally putting the spotlight on the genitals, as was done for the mouth. This would necessitate an all-out crash program of thirty- and sixty-second spots on our home TV screens, displaying vaginas puffing away sophisticately on Tiparillos, sipping Pink Chablis and exchanging jet-set gossip; ramrod-straight penises in white trenchcoats popping suddenly out of helicopters to peddle Glad Bags. (These effects can be achieved by puppetry or animation.) Perhaps my approach is a shade too daring for TV at the moment, but who's to say it will not be a *fait accompli* in the near future? After all, the networks have begun to advertise those intimate feminine hygiene sprays to millions of viewers, a development that would have been unthinkable a while back. Now we are witnessing stunning blond goddesses from Hollywood and Broadway lauding the virtues of such products as Feminique, Bidette, Easy Day (my, didn't they come close to the mark with that name!), Vespre and FDS (whose initials suggest it was created solely for New Left Females). The advertising campaigns for these feminine hygiene products have been on the cautious side so far, doing little more than to suggest that the user will feel "all woman," but when the agencies concerned become bolder and go for the hard sell, they may have the following slogans free of charge with my compliments:

—"The couple that sprays together stays together. . . ."

—"Before you flirt, give it one little squirt. . . ."

—"Does she or doesn't she? Only her lover knows for sure. . . ."

—"One dash of our mist and you'll surely be kissed. . . ."

A splendid idea, these feminine sprays. I can hardly wait until they come out in a roll-on! And I predict—look who became Criswell all of a sudden—that male hygiene sprays will be next on the market. If Revlon, for instance, is interested in pulling off a coup, here are some sample product names, again gratis: "Wang Tang," "Cool Tool," "Balls O' Fire," "Slick Wick," "Peckerique" . . .

WE SEEM TO HAVE STRAYED FAR AFIELD FROM OUR HYPOTHETICAL COUPLE. THEY'VE CHECKED INTO A SLEAZY HOTEL; THEY'VE GUZZLED SOME WINO'S "SNEAKY PETE"; THEY'VE MADE AN ESCAPE ROPE BY KNOTTING THE BEDSHEETS; THEY'VE LOOKED AT, SMELLED, FELT, HEARD AND TASTED EACH OTHER. NOW WHAT?

Let them rest a while, send out for a couple of pastrami sandwiches, watch "The Big Broadcast of 1935" on Channel 13. What's the rush? There's plenty of time to fool around.

AND AFTER THE RESPITE?

The man utilizes all the techniques previously mentioned to get her worked up again, paying special attention to the clitoris and breasts. Incidentally, the former should not be rubbed in a hamhanded manner, else it will become too irritated to send its sensations rippling throughout her body. Far better to make gentle, teasing contact with the tip of a felt pen or a good grade of feather.

FROM WHAT KIND OF BIRD?

Goose. What else? He then performs nipplingus, taking care to run the tongue over the dark area encircling the nipple, called the aureole. (A classy touch here would be to croon Hoagy Carmichael's haunting ballad "Baltimore Aureole" directly into the area. Rumor has it the song was composed during a Blaze Starr strip show.)

SINCE WE'RE IN THE CHESTAL ZONE, TELL US: WHY ARE THERE ONLY TWO BREASTS ON A WOMAN'S BODY?

Because if women had three the Playtex people would go bankrupt trying to retool. Also remember that man was given two hands, one for cuddling each breast. If his lady love possessed three of those gorgeous globes, he might have a mental breakdown deciding which two of the trio to caress. One and Two? Two and Three? One and Three? What if the breast left unfondled was the real winner?

HER CLITORIS AND BREASTS ABLAZE, WHAT DOES HE DO NOW?

He artfully eases his erect penis into the vaginal orifice and, as she emits a shivery sigh, sinks his teeth into her neck, *drawing no more than 2 cc. of blood;* otherwise it becomes a very sick, vampirish business. As she experiences the sliding of his organ against her sensitive inner nerve-endings, she drums her fingers along his spinal column, picking out a fast-paced kind of Terry Gibbs vibraharp solo on his vertebrae.

WHAT TUNE DOES SHE CHOOSE?

"I've Got You Under My Skin." Then after exciting each other to the brink of madness with those hot terms I furnished before (saving, of course, "bulbospongiosum" for the walloping climax), they start a series of rhythmic strokes.

HOW MANY STROKES?

It depends on their orientation. If he is, *par exemple,* a former coxswain of the Yale racing crew he may thrust his penis into her at a rate of 47 to 62 strokes per minute and be enchanted at her fervent response: "Oh, darling, your boola-boola is heavy, heavy!" Perhaps she was once a Singer sewing machine operator in Manhattan's garment industry; hence she will needle him into 200 strokes per minute. Golf pros making love may slow it down to 96 strokes over a three-hour span, but enjoy it just as much. (HE: "Oh, Mickey, you do it so Wright! I love being in your rough; I love your trap!" SHE: "Baby, slip that Rodriguez to me again! I dig your driver! I love your putts!") The highest number of strokes recorded during sex was 7,000 per minute by Duane Jones, an automobile mechanic schooled in high-compression; the lowest one, by Otis Beeler of Mahwah, New Jersey. His single stroke, sad to say, was a coronary.

ARE THERE ANY METHODS FOR PROLONGING THE ACT?

Three. The first, an involuntary method, is called *coitus interruptus.*

WHAT DOES IT MEAN?

It's Latin for "Dammit, Selma, the phone is ringing!" and it happens all too frequently. I have a theory that those wild-eyed individuals who hurl firebombs at Bell Telephone offices are not Weathermen or any other sort of revolutionaries, just people seeking revenge for telephonic intrusions on their swinging. Secondly, we have a technique, Karezza, which can best be described as immobile intercourse (humping without pumping). The couple, having coupled, just lie there for hours at a time sans movement. This can be very irritating to the testicles of the male, which if unrelieved by orgasm, are subject to a horrible ache known to the lower classes as "blue balls," to people of refinement as "azure agates." The third method is a new one called "Vietnam".

WHAT IS "VIETNAM"?

Just as he begins to escalate, she dovishly demands a pull-out. But these methods of prolongation are frustrating. We've come too far along the road to raunchiness for our couple to waste time beating around the bush. What we want now is the satisfaction only orgasm can give.

HOW CAN THE LOVERS USE THEIR ORGANS TO BRING EACH OTHER TO ORGASM?

The male should be driving into his partner in several ways, straight-forwardly and at various angles so that his instrument is impacting against all the sweet goodies: vulva, clitoris, cervix and silex. In and out, in and out, in and out . . . and her vaginal muscles clasp his penis, then unclasp, clasp, unclasp, clasp, unclasp, clasp, unclasp. . . .

DOCTOR, DO YOU THINK THAT . . . DOCTOR? DOCTOR?

. . . clasp, unclasp, clasp, unclasp, clasp, unclasp . . .

DOCTOR? DOCTOR?

. . . clasp, unclasp, unclasp . . . oh, mercy . . . I slipped a clasp somewhere in there and it was probably one hell of a clasp, if I know my clasps.

DOCTOR, THERE'S A FARAWAY LOOK IN YOUR EYES. HAVE YOU HYPNOTIZED YOURSELF?

A momentary lapse. You'll forgive a middle-aged man his memories, won't you? What's your next question?

WHAT IS MUTUAL ORGASM?

An insurance company in Omaha.

A REAL KNEE-SLAPPER, DOCTOR? SERIOUSLY, WHAT IS MUTUAL ORGASM?

The simultaneous coming (our reserved British cousins would say "arriving") or sexual climax. If the love partners can achieve it again, it is called The Second Coming. (I *told* you sex and religion are natural allies.)

IS MUTUAL ORGASM DESIRABLE?

Oh yes. It would be emotionally gratifying if each knew the other had undergone the same fantastic sensation at precisely the same instant, but it doesn't always happen. Sometimes he comes and she doesn't; sometimes she comes and he doesn't. As long as they both come eventually, it doesn't matter. If neither comes, it does matter. This we call "impotence"—nature's way of saying you're in for a rotten night—and it's our next topic.

CHAPTER SIX

IMPOTENCE: POLAR PENISES AND ICEBOXES

Impotence is nothing more (and nothing less; one should be quite precise in giving scientific definitions) than the failure of the penis and/or vagina to perform properly during the sexual act. In alley argot impotent males are called "no-pops," impotent females "cold cuts." I prefer the word "dysfunction."

WHAT IS THE DERIVATION OF THE WORD "DYSFUNCTION"?

One of my first field clinics was opened in the Bensonhurst section of Brooklyn, New York, a colorful subculture noted for its linguistic peculiarities. Whenever I would ask a Bensonhurst native to explain his or her problem, he or she would blush and say, "Cheez, Doc, I'm havin' a lotta trouble wit', uh, dis function. Dis function ain't functionin' nohow." I found that Bensonhurst residents, ordinarily quite outspoken about other aspects of life, turned strangely shy when conversing about sex, referring to it obliquely as "dis function." So I learned when dealing with them to use their euphemism, later substituting for the "i" in "dis" a "y," which gave the word a touch of class. It is interesting to note that had I begun my investigations in the Bronx the word would have evolved to "datfunction."

WHAT IS THE MAJOR REASON FOR DYS- OR DATFUNCTION?

That most unpredictable sector of human anatomy, the mind. Let me give you a case history illustrative of how the mind can cause sexual hangups. H.T. and his wife, W.T., (these are not the true initials; I use fictive ones to shield them from embarrassment, being a firm subscriber to the Gentleman's Code) were in dire straits, intercourse-wise. Married thirteen years, neither had experienced orgasm in all that time. Their bedroom life was an absolute horror. Night after night their sexual tissues screamed for relief, and there is nothing more agonizing than the sound of screaming tissues. (Neighbors three block away heard them every night and commented to each other: "By God, there go those screaming tissues again!")

To get his mind off his unfulfilled cravings, Mr. T. read endlessly from the lengthy works of Hugo and Dumas, deriving little or no enjoyment for he knew not a word of French. She, when the urge came upon her, checked it by devoting herself to knitting sweaters. She completed one whole sweater every night for thirteen years.

About once a month their eyes would meet furtively, flash an unmistakable message *(let's try again)*, and they did, hoping desperately that this time the act would bring on orgasm. Alas, it was as exciting as a soggy Tootsie Roll hitting nine-day-old turkey stuffing.

One night the T.'s could stand it no longer. Summoning up maniacal strength, they crashed through the towering barrier of 4,745 sweaters into the street and staggered to my office. A sorry sight they were, two people flushed by exertion, wool skeins dangling from their limbs, a No. 6 knitting needle sticking out of his navel. . . .

BEFORE THEY DECIDED TO SEEK YOUR ADVICE, HADN'T THEY READ ANY OF THE BEST-SELLING SEXUAL MANUALS ON THE MARKET?

To be sure, but to no avail. Let us see why. Masters and Johnson can be dispensed with quickly. This duo published in 1966 a book called *Human Sexual Response*. Then in 1970 they brought out a sequel, *Human Sexual Inadequacy*. It took them four years to determine that people don't know how to ball. These are experts by you?

HOW ABOUT DR. DAVID REUBEN?

Well, he takes a pleasant enough photo on his book's dust jacket, but the caption underneath tips off his worth by telling us he has a private psychiatric practice in San Diego. One would assume, if Dr. Reuben is half as good as he claims, his community would have been straightened out by now. But if you know this nation as I do, you know that nobody associates sex with San Diego. The Zoo and Sea World, yes, but not sex. Exit Dr. David Reuben.

WASN'T *THE SENSUOUS WOMAN* HELPFUL TO THE DISTAFF HALF OF YOUR IMPOTENT COUPLE?

Of all the sexual authors currently raking in the coin, "The Sensuous Woman," known mysteriously as "J," has to be the most outrageous. Incidentally, I read her book and I know why she put down the solitary letter "J." She was too bushed from all her affairs to write out her full name.

"J's" program for sexual improvement is just plain daft. For openers, she counsels her henna-ed clientele to develop tactility (I don't use obfuscating words like this; "sense of touch" is good enough for people like you and me, the kind who made America what it is today) by putting on blindfolds and letting their fingers roam over the typical objects to be found in an American kitchen: tepid water in a soup dish, a toaster, a sprig of cauliflower, cleanser, Josephine the Plumber, etc. I spot at least two flaws in this approach: (A) A woman who, while exploring her kitchen environment manually, touches a hot oven door won't be in the mood for sex for a long time; (B) A woman who has conditioned her fingers to feel lustful at the touch of tepid water in a soup dish, a toaster, a sprig of cauliflower, cleanser, Josephine the Plumber, etc. may discover in a genuine sexual situation her lover's body turns her off because it doesn't remind her of tepid water in a soup dish, a toaster, a sprig of cauliflower, cleanser, etc. (Josephine the Plumber, maybe; I never trusted her.)*

Another of her exercises in sensuality consists of priming the tongue for love by sticking it out vio-

---

* Here's a bit of information Josephine doesn't tell her adoring TV fans. Only new Comet can take away the stains left by old Comet.

lently, swishing it in circles and finally licking the tip of the nose with it. Let some woman be caught doing this exercise and they'll clap leg irons on her and haul her away to Whitecoat, Pennsylvania.

"J" also believes in leaving sexy notes around the house for husbands just home from a business trip. "I'm warm and tingly now that you're home. Go to the refrigerator and drink a Martini I've left for you." A gross blunder. The fridge is the last place in the world to send a typically obese American spouse. Three kielbasa sandwiches on hard torpedo roll and a six-pack of Budweiser (Martini hell!) and he's off to the TV and Johnny Unitas and all thoughts of sex are buried by the Colts' front four.

Let us allow "J" some latitude and concede that the returning husband skips the caloric blandishments of his Amana. Note Two, taped to the bathroom mirror, apprises: "You have the most exciting body I've ever seen. Come to the bedroom." If he is an honest man, he goes to the bedroom, yanks his mate out of the sack and drives her straight to the optometrist, for any broad who sees in his collection of foam rubber bolsters an "exciting body" requires optical correction immediately.

Even squirrelier than her trail of notes are "J's" oral sex techniques. A woman is supposed to spread a thick coating of whipped cream on her lover's penis before paying it lip service, but I submit that any man who in the dim light of the boudoir sees a hot-eyed frau advancing upon his pelvis with an aerosol can in her hand is apt to scream in abject horror: "For heaven's sake, Helen, don't shave me there, not there!"

There is also the excellent chance that a woman will get to like the taste of the canned Reddi-Whip far better than *his* Reddi-Whip, and what happens to the romance then? Adieu, "J," and don't call us; we'll call you.

WE CAN SEE WHY YOU DESPISE THOSE "EXPERTS." GETTING BACK TO THE DYSFUNCTIONAL MR. AND MRS. T., YOU SAID THEIR PROBLEMS WERE ROOTED IN THE MIND. HOW DID YOU STRAIGHTEN THEM OUT?

It took only a few shrewd questions to put the finger on their quandary. Before their marriage they had coupled often, eagerly and well in the rear seat of his 1946 Dodge, generally on lonely roads or at drive-ins. Their excitement centered about the fact they were making love *al fresco* and exposing themselves to arrest by nosey police flashing their lights into the darkened automobile. When the union was legalized, these illicit thrills were taken away, and the mind perversely refused to permit gratification under normal, humdrum circumstances.

WHAT DID YOU DO ABOUT IT?

I set about recreating the atmosphere in which their genitalia had performed so well in the premarital stage. If making love *al fresco* in a 1946 Dodge would unblock the dysfunction, so be it. Locating that year and make was no easy task, but one of my chums is an antique auto dealer, whose name just happens to be Al Fresco, and he unearthed one from under a pile of scrap in Weehawken, New Jersey. The T.s, when they fully comprehended my game plan, gladly kicked in the few thousand necessary for restoration and clapped their palms in glee when they heard I had commissioned one of America's outstanding painters, Earl Scheib, to refinish the vehicle at the unheard of special price of $29.95. I had my tailor clothe them in the styles of their youth, zoot suit and twelve-foot watch chain for him, "New Look" midi and high-heeled anklestraps with platform soles for her, and bade them good luck as their jallopy, its Fluid Drive clicking merrily, chugged toward an old haunt outside of town. To add further authenticity, I, without their foreknowledge, got Al Fresco and his cousin, Al Dente, to impersonate state troopers and skulk about the Dodge, their flashlights playing on the naked lovers in the back-seat, who were also playing on the back seat. That midnight the T.'s experienced the thundering climaxes of yore and have continued to do so, except for those brief periods they have had to spend in jail and hospital, for indecent exposure and double pneumonia respectively.

SO YOUR CONTENTION IS THERE IS NO IMPOTENCE, THAT IT'S ALL IN THE MIND?

No doubt of it. There are a few physical impairments that can hinder intercourse, but, generally speaking, the mind is the culprit. Here's another case history to prove my theory:

Zenobia, aged 27, had never reached a climax in eight years of wedded life to 31-year-old Mortimer Clodd of 35678 Gaping Gerbil Road, Youngstown, Ohio (phone: YZ 747-8001).

THOSE ARE FICTIVE NAMES, OF COURSE, TO PROTECT THE PARTIES FROM EMBARRASSMENT.

No. When they're late with their payments I generally use real names. To press on, Zenobia's constant failures in bed had engendered in her a feeling of total ennui.

HOW DO YOU KNOW SHE WAS SO COMPLETELY BORED WITH SEX?

When a husband is making passionate love to his wife and she responds by nibbling a peach, calling a girlfriend long distance and typing a long, querulous letter to a divorce lawyer—during the act—this smacks of boredom to me.

PROOF ENOUGH. WHAT WAS ZENOBIA'S HANGUP?

Zenobia Clodd, my thorough psychological workup revealed, was deeply in love with her 50-year-old father, Randolph, who represented to her all that was truly masculine and powerful, and poor Mortimer, only five-three and 125 pounds, shriveled and bespectacled, could in no way match Randolph's image. At one point Zenobia had even considered marrying her father, but decided against it.

WHY?

Her mother was still alive. It could have gotten messy.

WHAT WAS YOUR TREATMENT?

If Zenobia could only be turned on by a father figure, a father figure she would have to have. Rummaging through her purse for my fee, I discovered and cleverly palmed a snapshot of dear old dad, a Herculean figure in his skimpy hiphuggers. I went to one of those novelty firms, had it blown up to real-life proportions, backed it with cardboard and cut out a hole in the groin. The same night, at my bidding, Mortimer dimmed the lights, stripped off his clothes, crouched behind the mockup, inserted his penis through the aperture into his wife and she became so excited she had six full orgasms, three partial orgasms and one acceptable near miss. "Oh, Mortimer," she sighed, "my heart belongs to daddy, but my part belongs to you." So if you everhear a man referred to contemptuously as a "cardboard lover," think of Mortimer Clodd and the swell times he's having, and take it with a grain of saltpeter.

A BRILLIANT THERAPY, DOCTOR. IMPOTENCE, TRULY, MUST BE MOSTLY IN THE MIND. BUT YOU DID MENTION THERE WERE SOME PHYSICAL IMPAIRMENTS RESPONSIBLE FOR IT. CAN YOU ELABORATE?

In five per cent of women there is a condition that

can bring on pain whenever intercourse is attempted. This we call "dyspareunia." Just to see this word in print is daunting for it is formed from the ugliest collection of syllables in your Funk & Wagnalls. Not only is it revolting to look at but its very verbal usage can bring pain to the speaker, the pronunciation often forcing the teeth into distorted positions in which it shreds the tongue into strips. Say "dyspareunia" a couple of times and you'll see.

DYSPAREUNIA, DYSP—OH, DOCTOR, WE'VE SCORED OUR TONGUE AND THE INSIDE OF THE MOUTH. WHY DIDN'T YOU CLASH YOUR TONGUE WHEN YOU PRONOUNCED IT?

Because I knew what was coming and had the foresight to jam some cotton wads in there. When a woman has dysp—oh, mercy, the damn cotton must have fallen out; I'm bleeding like a pig—when a woman has it, the vagina becomes too tautly clamped around the penis, making withdrawal difficult if not impossible. A man atop a woman with this condition gets more of a screwing than he bargained for. I know of a case where three interns had to lift and turn the man counter-clockwise eighty times before he could be extricated.

WHAT CAN MAN DO TO COMBAT THIS PROBLEM?

If he suspects his bedmate is plagued by excessive vaginal constriction he should douse his organ before penetration with liberal amounts of some oleaginous substance to facilitate painless removal. To attain this desired slipperiness, some men use butter, the high-priced spread. I personally see nothing wrong in using less expensive Chiffon margarine. However, if the woman herself is a high-priced spread, it's more elegant to use the butter.

There are two other maladies which can cause impotence, but they are so exceedingly rare and their names so disgusting that I won't list them. Anyway we've proved conclusively that impotence is primarily a mind-related phenomenon. If you can free the mind you free the body.

WOULDN'T IT BE WONDERFUL IF THE THERAPY THAT FREES THE MIND WAS ITSELF FREE OF THE EXCESSIVE FEES YOU DOCTORS GET?

One more smartass remark like that and I'll make you pronounce you know what thirty times until your entire jaw is mutilated.

DOCTOR, UNTIL NOW WE'VE CONCERNED OURSELVES WITH PEOPLE WHO MAKE LOVE TO OTHER PEOPLE, BUT AREN'T THERE THOSE WHO MAKE LOVE WITHOUT OTHER PEOPLE?

Yes, the who-needs-you crowd that practices masturbation, our next chapter subject.

CHAPTER SEVEN

MASTURBATION: THE LONE HAND RIDES AGAIN!

DOCTOR, WE'VE HEARD SO MANY LURID TALES ABOUT MASTURBATION AND ITS EFFECTS, FOR INSTANCE, CAN CONSTANT MASTURBATION CAUSE PROFUSE GROWTH OF HAIR IN THE HAND?

Let me cite the case of Dudley G., who has been masturbating five times a day since he was eight years old. Dudley G. is the only person I know who goes to a manicurist for a wash and set. A hearty handshake from Dudley is a curious experience; it's rather like pressing a beard, and after you pull your hand away you have to scrape off a glistening layer of dandruff. His chronic habit has caused him a spate of difficulties. Before she read Dudley's lifeline, Madame Antonescu, the gypsy fortuneteller, was forced to shave his palm. Purchasing gloves is another problem. His left hand takes a normal size nine, but only a catcher's glove can accommodate his right or "action" hand. (This has earned Dudley the sobriquet of "Yogi.") Perhaps, though, Dudley will eventually cut down on his masturbatory activity due to encroaching old age, for the hair in his hand definitely shows streaks of gray.

CAN MASTURBATION CAUSE BLINDNESS?

Dudley quizzed me on that very point some weeks ago, but I assured him it was a myth. He emitted a relieved sigh, thanked me warmly, and strode out of my office, tripping heavily over a slight fold in the carpet. It could have been a nasty fall, save for Rollo whose lightning reflexes blocked it.

WHO IS ROLLO?

His seeing eye dog, a noble beast worth his weight in Gainesburgers.

CAN IT LEAD TO INSANITY?

Of all the canards swirling about masturbation this has to be the most risible. A group of heavy masturbators heard me broach it during a recent therapy session and they laughed so hard they tipped over their highchairs and fell into a collection of documents outlining their plan to take over the entire solar system in twenty-four hours. Incidentally, I've seen their plan; it's positively brilliant, and should be executed like clockwork as soon as they discover a way to get a little more speed out of their dune buggies.

WHEN DOES IT START?

At 1800 hours on 23 February, 1974. The first assault team will hit and secure Venus, Neptune and Saturn, followed by—

NO, DOCTOR. WE DON'T MEAN THE TAKE-OVER OF THE SOLAR SYSTEM. WHEN DOES MASTURBATION START?

Usually in very young children. Mother unwittingly introduces them to it when she soaps their genitals during the daily bath. Discovering pleasure in the rub-a-dub-dub, some ingenious toddlers will deliberately rush outside and roll around in the mire, knowing *maman* will be compelled to bathe them again. I know of one little fellow who went through sixteen cases of Camay before mummy got hip.

One of the legendary methods of masturbation came about through the marketing of that grand old toy of bygone days, the Erector Set—and how aptly that device was named! A boy would tie one end of a string around one of the Erector's moving parts, the other to his penis, switch on the power, lie back and feel it go up and down, up and down, up and down, up and down . . .

DOCTOR, WE SEEM TO HAVE—DOCTOR? DOCTOR?

. . . up and down, up and down, up and down, up and down . . .

DOCTOR, THAT MISTY LOOK IS ON YOUR FACE AGAIN. . . .

Again, a thousand pardons for that revisitation to Memory Lane. Golly, we guys loved that old Erector Set and the way it made men of us. It just wasn't the same with a Lionel train.

THE ERECTOR SET WAS FINE FOR BOYS, BUT WHAT DID GIRLS USE?

Young girls suddenly aware of sexual sensation used a variety of penile substitutes: turnips, parsnips, cucumbers (happily not as cool as they were supposed to be!), carrots (these girls knew what was up, doc!), squash, etc. A mature woman who fondly recalls her "salad days" may also have a misty look on her face.

WERE BANANAS EVER USED?

No, the vagina was no place for a banana split. As women progress they generally abandon the produce counter and take up more sophisticated novelties, among them the dildoe, nothing more than an artificial penis of plastic or rubber, and the far more fascinating internal stimulator from the Orient, the *ben-wa*. This consists of two silver balls about the size of a small plum, one hollow, the other partly filled with mercury.

KNOWING WHAT WE DO TODAY ABOUT POLLUTION, ISN'T THE BALL WITH THE MERCURY POTENTIALLY DANGEROUS?

If the masturbator is a female tuna, yes.

HOW IS THE BEN-WA UTILIZED?

In a manner that would have gladdened the heart of the late Rube Goldberg. The woman (A) reclines in a rocking chair (B) and begins a steady back and forth swaying, inserts the hollow ball (C) deeply into the vagina (D), and the mercury ball (E) in front of the hollow ball. The rocking causes the mercury in the outer ball to slide around and make the outer ball collide with the inner ball, which, in turn, touches the cervix (F). The aroused cervix radiates sensual vibrations to the clitoris (G), vulva (H), and labia (I). The sensation mounts even higher and at the exact moment the woman is completely off her rocker, orgasm takes place. These silver *ben-wa* balls are called "Queegs" in this country in memory of Captain Queeg, the immortal paranoid of Herman Wouk's best-selling novel *The Caine Mutiny*, who went about clacking two similar silver spheroids in his agitated hands, and they could cause his kind of mental anguish to the user in rare instances. A woman clacking these balls around in her vagina who begins glowering and muttering darkly about the theft of frozen strawberries should be separated from these silver balls immediately and placed under sedation.

But the instrumentality that has truly won the hearts and lower parts of woman is the vibrator, a penis-shaped affair with the added kicker of a motor. Many women report remarkable masturbatory experiences with vibrators, but two basic problems keep cropping up.

WHAT ARE THESE PROBLEMS WITH THE VIBRATOR?

The first derives from the fact that women by nature are more emotional about sex than men. To support this claim let me quote the words of Harry B., a patient of mine: "Dr. Weinstein, my Marion has this wild idea that when I'm making love to her she should hear a thousand violins playing—a thousand violins! And that's why I can't enjoy sex because right in the middle of it I'm thinking to myself, 'Where in the hell am I going to get the money to pay all those damn musicians on the patio?'"

YOUR POINT IS WELL TAKEN. WE CONCEDE THAT WOMEN ARE MORE EMOTIONAL THAN MEN, BUT HOW DOES THIS RELATE TO THE VIBRATOR?

Overly emotional women have been known to fall madly in love with vibrators, foolishly forgetting that they're mere inanimate objects. "You never talk to me after we have sex," one typical female whined to her vibrator. "I'm a live, vital woman who needs affection and understanding, not a cold, unfeeling machine.

Oh, I'm sorry about that last remark. I didn't mean to get personal."

HOW CAN THE VIBRATOR FULFILL THE WOMAN'S EMOTIONAL NEEDS?

Quite simply by telling her it loves her. And this can be achieved if the firms manufacturing these contraptions heed my advice and augment them with one significant improvement: tiny cassettes housed somewhere inside which are capable of producing recorded voices. Here's what would occur: A vibrator, once informed by its sensors that a woman has come to climax, would activate the cassette setup and begin to murmur, "I love you for yourself, not just for your beautiful body. This is no one-night stand, no summer romance that withers in the first autumnal chill. No, baby, this is you and me together forever, walking in the rain, touching the stars, and I swear by all the holy IBM circuits within me that I'll see you again and again in the city . . ." and similar banal, but always effective tripe.

EXCELLENT ADVICE AND WE HOPE THE MANUFACTURERS TAKE IT. WHAT'S THE SECOND VIBRATOR PROBLEM?

A gruesome one affecting only those vibrators powered by batteries. Premature expiration.

THAT SOUNDS AWFUL! WHAT IS PREMATURE EXPIRATION?

A battery, say, that's supposed to last until July conks out in May, perhaps even during a critical moment. You can perceive how grievous that could be. I do not wish to be put in the position of making commercial endorsements—unless I'm lavishly paid—but I must say that in sex a battery, like a woman, should be ... now get this ... Everready.

DOCTOR, IS MASTURBATION JUSTIFIABLE?

Yes. An individual may be friendless in a strange town, lacking the going love-for-sale price, fearful of meeting new people or contracting disease ... whatever ... so masturbation is the only tension reliever at hand. If you decide to do it, fine, but for the sake of common decency don't be ... *pushy*. That is, don't make a schoolboyish grab for yourself. That would be uncouth and low-class. Consider: If you were trying to seduce another person, wouldn't you be at your witty, scintillating, *soignee* best? Of course! So why defraud yourself, the dearest person you know, of the same treatment? Remember, *you're* your date this evening! Take yourself out to an expensive French restaurant; take yourself out to a hit musical; then, upon returning to your room, take yourself out.

Whisper thrilling endearments to yourself. "I love you, I love you, heaven knows I love you" ... and mean it. Steal a glance in the mirror; isn't that face, that fabulous face, aglow; aren't those eyes furtively acknowledging, "Yes, yes, I surrender, but please, please be kind. . . ."?

Choosing the proper hand lotion is a must. Again, don't be pushy and disrespectful by trying to fob off on yourself some garish cut-rate drugstore emulsion. Use cool and creamy Jergen's if you're an effete urban snob, bracing and hearty Corn Huskers if you're a rugged prairie type. Work the lotion in slowly and lovingly; make those lifelines shine; watch the hand clenching in desire. Before lying down, place on the stereo (we must assume that all experienced travelers carry a stereo) an album expressly recorded to accompany the act, "Monte Carlo, Moonlight and Masturbation." (This we call adult or middle-of-the-road music. Another, less ethereal LP, "Let's Do The Jerkaloo," covers the rock crowd.)

The songs have been selected to complement the physical action from first caress to final splat. A chorus opens with the romantic advice, "Sit there . . . and move your little fingers"; an Eddie Fisher-type baritone thunders, "with this hand . . . I will work for yo-o-o-o-u!"; a sly folksinger twangs, "It's a treat to beat yo' meat on de Mississippi mud . . ." and so on until the grand finale: A Jamaican steel drum band exhorting the blurring fist on to the pounding, pulsating climax with that raucous old Calypso tune:

> Jack! Jack! Jack!
> Cu Cu Tu Gu Ru Gu!
> Jack! Jack! Jack!
> Cu Cu Tu Gu Ru Gu!
> Jack! Jack! Jack!

DOCTOR, THAT MANIACAL GLEAM IS IN YOUR EYE AGAIN! AND WHAT DOES "CU CU TU GU RU GU" MEAN?

I don't know and I don't care. Jack! Jack! Jack! Cu Cu Tu—

DOCTOR! DOCTOR! SAY SOMETHING!

Ah-h-h-h-h-h. . . .

CHAPTER EIGHT

PERVERSIONS: THE FAG BAG, MACK THE DYKE AND OTHER DANDY DEVIATIONS

DOCTOR, WHAT IS A FAG?

A guy who takes another guy out to lunch. These tragic homosexual men, who express sexual interest only in members of their own sex, also are termed fairies, queers, queens, swish, feathers, nancy boys, sissy boys, gay boys and bromosexuals.

WHAT IS A BROMOSEXUAL?

A fag with a constant migrain.

WHERE CAN YOU FIND HOMOSEXUALS?

Generally, right behind you. Actually, they can be found all over: public libraries, Turkish baths, beauty parlors, rice paddies, tundras, coal mines, ski lifts, opium dens, hamburger joints and, most frequently, lurking about in men's rooms, called, in homosexual jargon, "penile colonies."

WHAT MAKES THEM THE WAY THEY ARE?

Their early life in the home. A domineering mother keeps her son tied too closely and long to her apron strings; he tends to identify with her instead of his father; he turns homosexual. A father is so ultra-masculine that his son is beset by insecurity; he feels he'll never be half the man Dad is, so why even try?; he turns homosexual. A thoughtful mother and father raise their boy in a tranquil, balanced way; they make no unreasonable demands that could cause undue anxiety; free of pressures, he knows and enjoys his role in the family, the community, the nation, the cosmos; he turns homosexual.

Happily married men may also be transformed into homosexuals, ironically enough by their wives. A man may desire frequent sexual relations and his wife, playing amateur psychologist, says, "Why all the sex action? You trying to hide your latent homosexuality by being overly masculine?" So he diminishes his sexual activity drastically, whereupon she complains, "You don't attack me as often as you used to. Are you a latent homosexual?" So he says, "the hell with it"; he turns homosexual!

TURNING TO THE OPPOSITE SEX, WHAT'S YOUR ANALYSIS OF LESBIANS?

Lesbians to me are as good as any other group of immigrants. They came here on stinking cattleboats seeking a new purpose, a new life; they bent their backs in the boiling desert sun, built a shining ribbon of steel that linked New York harbor and Frisco, fought and died so you and I could be free. Anyway, who am I to look down my nose at Lesbians, Albanians, Armenians, Lithuanians? My own forbears fled the hell holes of Russia to come here. I say: give me your tired, your poor, your huddled masses, your wreached refuse, I lift my lamp beside the golden door. . . .

ARE HOMOSEXUALS EASY TO SPOT?

It depends on a number of variables. Do homosexuals, when you aim the spray can at them, jump lithely to one side and avoid the jet or do they hold still? Are you using the proper color for the spotting? (White paint on white skin, for instance, won't show up at all.) If the paint is the right color, is it a good grade that will adhere to their skins or a cheap one easily washed off by a driving rain? Until I know the answers to these questions, I must decline to make a judgment.

LET'S REPHRASE THAT ONE. ARE HOMOSEXUALS EASY TO IDENTIFY?

Yes, if you run across individuals flaunting their homosexuality, i.e., the broad-shouldered, chunky, mannish "Butch" (the Lesbian in the male role) cracking boulders in her armpits, or the highly effeminate, shrieking, mincing "drag queen" in his gaudy finery. (Incidentally, did you ever mince a drag queen? It's wild. You preheat the oven at 375 degrees, take three quarts of lentils and one drag queen . . . oh, hell, let Julia Childs finish it; that's what she gets paid for.)

But there are homosexuals who wouldn't fit those clichés in a million years. (Maybe a million years; who knows what the species will look like by then?). One of the most masculine appearing men I ever met is a super-slugger for a West Coast big league baseball team. Off the field he's a switch hitter, too. There is a strikingly beautiful Hollywood actress who is as far from looking "dikey" as I am from good writing, yet she despises men with a passion and admits to ardent Lesbian affairs.

YOU'RE A TEASE, DOCTOR. YOU KNOW WE ALL LOVE A SCANDALOUS TIDBIT. WON'T YOU GIVE US A HINT AS TO THIS MOTION PICTURE LOVELY'S IDENTITY?

Well, just a hint, but nothing more. We're good friends and I wouldn't want to hurt her. I will say that you've seen her in several technicolor cartoons from the drawing boards of Disney, Lantz and Hanna-Barbera.

OH, YOU MEAN—

Shush! We've said enough.

WHAT DO MALE HOMOSEXUALS DO?

They masturbate and fellate each other and sometimes stimulate the anal passage by inserting either the penis or some other object.

OH, YES. WE RECALL DR. REUBEN'S BOOK QUOTING AN INTERN WHO HAD TO REMOVE A SHOT GLASS FROM A HOMOSEXUAL'S ANUS SHOVED IN BY ANOTHER HOMOSEXUAL.

I hate to keep downgrading Dr. Reuben, but I checked out that particular story. The man with the shot glass ass was not a homosexual at all, just a bartender who had figured out a clever, albeit uncomfortable way of smuggling expensive shot glasses out of his place of employment.

WHAT DO FEMALE HOMOSEXUALS DO?

Mutual masturbation with fingers or dildoes, mutual cunnilingus, etc. Much of this activity takes place at a gay bar.

WHAT IS A GAY BAR?

An institution for homosexual lawyers. Also a place for perverts to meet, drink and make assignations.

HAVE YOU EVER VISITED A GAY BAR?

Yes. To authenticate my research on this chapter I paid a visit to the Will O' the Lisp, a bistro in the heart of the notorious Selma Avenue lavender-light district in Hollywood frequented by homosexuals of both sexes. I had donned skintight Levi's, hobnailed boots and a black leather motorcycle jacket and crash helmet to make myself sartorially acceptable to the patrons, for I knew well the gay slogan, "Show me a guy in bike gear and I'll show you an Easy Rider."

I had been warned to expect the unusual, so I did not even flinch when a reedy figure in an oil-stained Texaco station attendant's uniform sidled up and whispered, "You can trust your car with the man who wears the bra. . . ." On stage Chief Youngtongue and the Sweet Sioux, the tribal rock band, evoked swoons and screams when they broke into:

> And now, my end is near,
> And I can see that you're excited.
> My dear, why not turn queer?
> I promise you, you'll be delighted,
> You'll have a thrilling trip,
> By traveling down my own sweet highway,
> Advance, take out your lance,
> And do it . . . my way. . . .

A gentle tugging at my elbow broke the music's spell. "Care to dance?" A slim, willowy maid in a breathtaking mini smiled up at me. "OK," I grunted. (My grunt is so realistic that I heard several patrons whisper, "Oh, there's a cop in here!") Alas, my lips brushing her cheek found some stubby ten o'clock shadow, and it was soon apparent that "she" was a "he." Rejecting her entreaties and an invitation to a pad in the Hollywood Hills, I disengaged, only to be gathered into the plump arms of another female.

"Please dance with me," the newcomer said in a plaintive way, and my ears pricked up (the reverse also occurred); they'd caught the tonal quality of a true woman in her voice, yet I bade my heart to be cautious; some of these female impersonators had uncanny talents for mimicry. "I don't make the fag scene, baby," I admonished her. "Thank heaven," she breathed. "I'm a Lesbian and I can tell from the cut of your clothes and your manly swagger that you are too. Listen, if my 'butch' knew I was two-timing him, she'd put a shiv in my back. But I can't help it. You're the grooviest bulldike I've ever seen. Let's you and me slip out and . . ."

"Shove off, you doubledealing bitch!" A flailing hand sent the girl out of my arms and against the phone booth. Her jealous "butch" had, indeed, witnessed the attempted betrayal and was prepared to do something about it. I caught a glint of steel in a gnarled hand and my knees trembled. A show of force was necessary. "Something on your mind?" I barked. (My bark is as lifelike as my grunt; the same patrons whispered, "The cop must have brought along his German shepherd.") The butch put away the shiv. "I like you," he-she said. "You got guts. Know what? I'm damn sick and tired of chasin' after this baggage over here. I always had a yen to make it with a fellow bulldike. What say, buddy? A plate of spaghetti at my place, a bottle of Cold Duck . . ."

Begging off because of the "curse," I moseyed away from the disappointed butch but was caught in midstride on the dance floor by a handsome, wavy-haired gent in a Borsalino jacket.

"Hi, I'm Norton Follansbee. Gay, of course, but fed up to here"—he indicated an anatomical location

—"with those shrill, clawing queens. With them the game isn't worth the candle, if you know what I mean. I can see you're a 'masculine gay' like me, so what say to a foxtrot or two, then a snack at my digs on Sunset Boulevard. . . . ?"

As Follansbee's hand neared my knee, it was knocked roughly aside by a fifth individual bursting into our midst, his eyes rolling wildly, his lips trembling. "For God's sake," he pleaded, grabbing the lapels of my jacket, "help me! I'm from the Los Angeles County Water & Power Department and I'm 'straight.' I came here on an emergency call, and I've been propositioned by everything in the joint, including the kitchen sink, which gurgled something suggestive when I walked by. Dance me out the door and I'll do anything you want. Anything!"

Filled with deep pity for the man, I complied, waltzed him onto Selma Avenue, revealed that I, too, was a "straight" (a heterosexual), and we had a few beers, chatted about our narrow escape from the Will O' The Lisp, became fast friends and wound up the evening like real men—with a couple of hookers.

A HARROWING EXPERIENCE, DOCTOR, BUT WHAT DID IT PROVE?

Nothing really. My publisher told me to pad this section a little.

CAN PEOPLE CHANGE THEIR SEX THROUGH SURGICAL MEANS?

You've heard that old proverb, "You can't make a purse out of a sow's ear"? Well, all a Scandinavian medico does by operating is to turn a man with a penis into a man without a penis. A woman he'll never be. However, a really talented surgeon working from a photograph or drawing *can* transform a patient into a purse or a sow's ear, but it's expensive and always fatal.

LEAVING THE TORMENTED DENIZENS OF THE GAY WORLD, LET'S TURN TO ANOTHER SUBJECT. WHAT ARE SOME OF THE OTHER DEVIATIONS?

We have the foot fetishists (the Dr. Scholl syndrome) who must fondle women's toes, soles, and insteps. These deviants are also classified as archcriminals or Achilles' heels.

Peeping Toms are those pitiful men who crouch beneath a woman's window hoping to catch her undressing. This practice is generally harmless, both to peeper and peepee, but in one instance it proved fatal to the former. The woman lived on the 33rd floor.

The obsession of a pyromaniac (arsonist) with fire has a sexual basis. He gets his jollies by masturbating in the vicinity of the conflagrations he's set. One of my pyromaniacal patients ejaculated so profusely that he put out the fire.

Mirror freaks attach tiny mirrors to their toes, engage a woman in conversation, shove their feet under the dress for the purpose of viewing her private parts reflected in the glass. A particularly clever woman found a unique way of dealing with a mirror freak. She let him get close enough for a peek; he glanced down at his toe-mirror and shuddered. "YOU'RE UNDER ARREST" advised the words she had stenciled on her corset. Then she stepped on his foot, shattering the mirror, which brought him seven years of bad look.

Many a woman has been frightened out of her wits by a phone pervert, the gent who calls up with the heavy breathing and the string of obscene suggestions. Instead of panicking, here is how she should handle the next phone pervert:

WOMAN: Hello!

PHONE PERVERT: (breathing heavily) Aaaa ah, aaaaah ... you all alone, gorgeous?

WOMAN: I see. What would you like to do to me?

PHONE PERVERT: Aaaaaah, aaaaah, aaaaah, I'd like to rip off your flimsy ... aaaaah, aaaaah, aaaaah. ...

WOMAN: Yes, yes, my flimsy ... so sheer and diaphanous, revealing every curve, every hollow. ... Now you just keep talking and masturbating if you so desire. I especially want to hear that aaaaaah, aaaah again. I thought I detected a little something I didn't like in your breathing.

PHONE PERVERT: ... force you down on the couch and thrust my hand across your ... aaaaah, aaaaah ... hey, what do you mean you heard something in my breathing?

WOMAN: Yes, your hand across my ... so ablaze with desire, so milky and soft. ... Just let me hear that aaaaah, aaaah, aaaaah one more time, please.

PHONE PERVERT: Who the hell are you, lady?

WOMAN: You're a very fortunate young man. You've accidentally reached a prominent chest surgeon. I am Dr. Bertha Kneeshaw. Now, how long have you had that rattling in your chest? Not that it's anything too much to worry about. Fully sixteen per cent of those who exhibit your symptoms make dramatic recoveries and live as long as three months and you might be among the sixteen per cent. Think of it, ninety more days of precious life, but only if you hurry. After you relieve yourself, I suggest you make an appointment with me at West Valley Hospital. Right now; don't even bother to zip up your trousers. I'm a doctor and nothing shocks me. We can get the blood work and the pre-op stuff done in no time at all and you can be under the knife in twenty minutes. . . . Hello? *hello?* (Muses) I don't think he's going to come . . . ever.

CHAPTER NINE

ODDS AND ENDS, AND A VERY ODD END

DOCTOR, WE'VE BEEN TOSSING TOUGH QUESTIONS YOUR WAY FOR SEVERAL HOURS AND WE'RE AMAZED AT YOUR COURAGEOUS, FRANK RESPONSES.

I told you in my prefatory remarks I would be fearless and truthful. It's the only way to save my country from ignorance and doom.

WONDERFUL! NOW A FEW MORE QUESTIONS ON MISCELLANEOUS TOPICS AND WE'LL LET YOU GO BACK TO THE CLINIC. HOW DOES A PERSON CONTRACT VENEREAL DISEASE?

It's disgusting and I don't want to talk about it. A little ignorance and doom isn't all that bad.

COME, COME, DOCTOR. THERE'S NO HIDING FROM REALITY. HOW DOES ONE GET VENEREAL DISEASE?

One per cent of V.D. cases is attributable to intercourse, the other ninety-nine per cent to toilet seats. A person having intercourse *on* a toilet seat is really asking for it—a rash act that will surely culminate in a rash. Fortunately, the most prevalent of these afflictions—syphilis, gonorrhea and B.V.D. (a strain of V.D. caused by underwear)—are treated with antibiotics if detected in time.

HOW CAN V.D. BE DETECTED?

In its advanced stages rather easily. Arms, legs, heads, breasts, etc. break their moorings and fall off the body to the ground. However, a better method of detection is a blood test in the early stages. And remember, in my business plus-fours are not golfing knickers.

THANKS FOR THE TIP. TO BE FOREWARNED IS TO BE FOREARMED.

And to be forearmed (four-armed) is to have twenty fingers! We needed a little humor right here. V.D. is a depressing subject.

WHAT IS SODOMY?

Sodomy refers to unspeakably vile sexual acts between men and women or men and animals. The latter we also call bestiality. I want to go on record right now as saying I do not condone either horsing around or, as hillbillies are wont to do, puttin' with mutton or pulling the wool over one's eyes. And I also believe in that proverb: let sleeping dogs lie (with other sleeping dogs).

The term "sodomy" comes from the Biblical town of Sodom, which was destroyed along with its sister city, Gomorrah, by fire, because of their inhabitants' monumental wickedness. The same fate awaits Las Vegas, I have no doubt.

CAN WE NOT INFER, THEN, THAT THERE IS A PRACTICE CALLED "GOMORRAH-MY"?

There is, but I would not describe it in a book designed only as soft-core pornography. All I'll say is that it has something to do with a chicken, some petroleum jelly and a trampoline.

DOCTOR, WHAT IS AN ORGY?

A group of naked people who assemble for the purpose of failing at sex.

WHAT IS THE "RHYTHM METHOD"?

When a woman makes it with a pianist, bassist and drummer. It also means not having intercourse at certain times in the woman's menstrual cycle in order to avoid pregnancy. But it doesn't always work, as the message of this old popular song clearly tells us:

> I use rhythm,
> I use rhythm,
> I've got twelve kids,
> Who could ask for anything more?

WHAT IS AUTOEROTICISM?

In men, the urge to masturbate in Lincolns, Imperials or Cadillacs. In women, an urge to attack Ralph Williams.

WHAT IS ABORTION?

Termination of pregnancy, accidentally, by some physical defect in mother and/or child, or deliberately, by recourse to doctors or quacks.

SHOULD ABORTIONS BE LEGALIZED?

If women desire them, yes. Low-cost abortion supermarkets should be available to women all over the land. "Get your D & C at the A & P" should be their motto.

WHAT IS COPULATION?

Sex between consenting policemen. In this special sense, the word "cop-out" means a policeman in heat.

WHAT IS THE BEST SUBSTANCE TO RECLINE UPON FOR MAKING LOVE?

Astroturf.

WHAT IS A FRENCH TICKLER?

Jacques Tati.

SPANISH FLY?

A 470-foot clout by Orlando Cepeda. The term also means a drug manufactured from the body of the blister beetle of southern France and Spain. It could as well have been named "French fly," but the French already have loads of big-time credits—French toast, French bread. French dressing, French pastry, etc., so we gave the Spanish a break.

WHAT DOES SPANISH FLY DO?

It irritates the bladder and stimulates the sexual organs. But it is highly dangerous and *should never be used on a human being.* You have all heard the story of a Spanish-fly dosed woman who became so aroused that, after she wore out her boyfriend, she had intercourse with his automobile's parts.

YES, WE'VE HEARD THAT YARN. WHAT HAPPENED TO HER?

Still unsated, she ran across the street to a nearby used car lot (not Ralph Williams, incidentally) and in the next frenetic five minutes got heavy with a Chevy, cracked the back of a Pontiac, got her hands on a Toyota and ended up being gored by a Ford.

DIDN'T THIS RAMPAGE BRING ABOUT PHYSICAL DAMAGE TO HER?

Some, but a surgeon working hand in hand with an auto mechanic did the necessary repairs. Luckily, she was still under Blue Cross warranty.

EXCLUDING SPANISH FLY, ARE ANY OF THE APHRODISIACS EFFECTIVE IN PROMOTING SEXUALITY?

None of them. To increase our potency we've done some pretty horrible things: murdered rhinos for their allegedly aphrodisiacal horns, cut the testicles off bulls ("prairie oysters") and eaten them, chopped down spiderwort plants, killing both the spider *and* the wort, and feasted on dead bees, clams, oysters, expensive truffles, earthworms, etc. All to no avail. Many of us for years wolfed down Wheaties, the "Breakfast of Champions," another putative source of sexual vitality, until we found out recently it ranked very low on the breakfast cereal nutritional scale. "Breakfast of Chumps" would be more like it. If Wheaties had any sexual merits at all, the Rev. Bob Richards would have written this book, not I.

CAN DRUGS DO ANYTHING TO IMPROVE SEX LIFE?

If you mean marijuana and LSD, I would say that my personal experimentation with them during sex was a total bust. The bust came about 3 a.m. when the girl in my arms revealed she was a "nark" (narcotics agent).

I even went a step further, mixed LSD with STP, the oil additive ("the racer's edge"), had a number of elaborate sexual fantasies, but all of them were about Andy Granatelli. Forget drugs, my friends. Sex, which has been a wondrous thing for more than forty years, doesn't need them. And now we will turn in our hymnals to No. 128, "There Is Water in the River" . . . .

HAVE YOU EVER GONE TO A HOUSE OF ILL REPUTE?

Ordinarily a man of my charm and verve needn't resort to that, but I did just once, solely for the edification of my readers. I visited "Slit City" a *casa de coorvehs* in Nevada, where I was accorded VIP honors and given its most experienced lady of the evening, Tough Tuchus Tessie.

HOW DO YOU KNOW SHE WAS THE MOST EXPERIENCED ONE?

She had on a Black Garter Belt, while the novices wore white or tan. Frankly, I hated every hour of it. Looking ruefully at my member, I said, "What's a nice joint like you doing in a girl like this?", disengaged and left.

WHAT MAKES A PROSTITUTE?

Usually another prostitute. Deep down they hate men.

WE MEAN, HOW DOES A GIRL GET STARTED IN PROSTITUTION?

Once the good jobs at a McDonald's drive-in are taken, a girl has no other recourse. Let McDonald's hire more girls and prostitution will cease.

WHAT IS A CONDOM?

A device of thin rubber rolled over the penis to stop men from impregnating women or contracting disease. It got its name from Dixieland jazz star Eddie Condom who learned to use it in Paris and later popularized it in this country.

WHERE IS IT PURCHASED?

In condominiums. Sometimes drugstores.

WHAT BIRTH CONTROL DEVICES DO WOMEN USE?

The diaphragm, which is a kind of internal condom, the intra-uterine mechanism (sometimes this gets knocked for a loop), the oral Pill and the violent headache, as in "Neil, don't touch me, darling. I've got a violent headache"; still the best device around.

WHAT CAN YOU TELL US ABOUT THE CHASTITY BELT?

The Chastity Belt is a region in the Adirondack Mountains of New York State whose girls are noted for their purity and inexperience, as opposed to the neighboring Borscht Belt in the Catskill Mountains where they are not.

WHAT IS A "WET DREAM"?

A dream interrupted by gushers from a defective waterbed. I know of a man sleeping on the ninth floor of a hotel who drowned in his own bed. "Wet dream" also means a man waking from a very spicy nocturnal fantasy to find he has ejaculated. A "dry dream" is almost the same thing, except the man is impotent.

WHAT IS MENSTRUATION?

I do not plan to do any menstruation jokes. Period.

WHAT IS THE MENOPAUSE?

Just what it sounds like. When a woman has had too many men, it's time for a pause.

WHAT IS A NYMPHOMANIAC?

A tragic woman rushing daily from bed to bed, from affair to affair in a desperate bid to attain sexual happiness, but never finding it. In other words, your basic American housewife.

Her male counterpart is the satyr, but unlike the "nymph" he only runs amuck one day a week.

WE'RE AFRAID TO ASK, BUT WHAT DAY IS THAT?

Satyrday.

ON THAT FINAL NOTE, WE GUESS IT'S TIME TO BID ADIEU....

I bid you adieus and raise you one shalom....

... BID ADIEU TO THE SEXUAL MASTERPIECE OF ALL TIME, *EVERYTHING YOU NEVER WANTED TO KNOW ABOUT SEX—BUT I'LL TELL YOU ANYWAY.* WE DON'T KNOW HOW, SOL WEINSTEIN, Ph. V.D., WE, THE AMERICAN PUBLIC, CAN EVER THANK YOU ENOUGH FOR REPAIRING OUR TATTERED SEXUAL LIVES.

PLEASE, please, no plaudits, no hero worship. Just treat me the way you would treat any ordinary god.

You're free now, Mr. and Mrs. Joe Doakes, Mr. and Mrs. John Q. Public, Mr. and Mrs. Eddie Everyman, free of guilt, shame and fear. I put it all together for you, baby. Now rip off your garments and make it, make it, make it!

YES, YES, DOCTOR! WE'LL MAKE IT! WE'LL MAKE IT! WE'LL MAKE IT!

One small favor. . . .

ANYTHING, DOCTOR, ANYTHING.

Could I watch?